THE RETURN
of
JUDAH

THE RETURN of JUDAH

"Listen, God, to the voice of Judah. Bring him to his people; strengthen his grip, be his helper against his foes..."

ELIZABETH JAMES

ORIGAMI

Parrésia Publishers Ltd.
82, Allen Avenue, Ikeja, Lagos, Nigeria.
+2348154582178, +2348062392145
origami@parresia.com.ng
www.parresia.com.ng

ISBN: 978-978-995-400-1

Printed in Nigeria by Parrésia Press

For Atlanta.

ACKNOWLEDGEMENT

I will love to appreciate the Almighty God, for "in Him, I move and live and have my being 'and ' unto Him who is able to do exceeding abundantly above all we could think, ask and imagine." The revelations, imaginations and expansion of thoughts are His.

My late mother Alice Umoh taught me to read early with her lovely magazines, Hers and Woman's Own. My Stepfather, late Mr. Sylvanus Umoh who relentlessly bought Reader's Digest, which formed and shaped my Reading culture.

My Cousin, Mrs Bernadette Ekaiyang, for taking me to her office at the National Library in Calabar. I spent most of my holidays there building myself intellectually.

My Principal, Mrs Jaja and cousin Dr. Margaret Ndoma Egba for teaching me how to play Scrabble. This was a solid foundation to writing properly

My husband, Oku James, for his friendship, companionship, and love, augured the flow of creativity to write.

My Pastor, Rev Dr. Iniobong F. Udoh, whose ministry inspired the birth of this book.

My son Atlanta Ubokudom; the main instrument of my inspiration and preoccupation for this book. My major Critic and cheerleader, my first editor and muse.

My lifelong friend, Margaret Thacker, is a sincere friend

that sticks closer than a sister. Her loyalty and commitment are a celebration of good company; as a reader of good books, the craving to write ' our kind of books' has informed my writing taste.

Tonia Lawanson, my editor, very practical and pushful. Her enthusiasm and encouragement are unrivalled when I had problems writing. If it were possible, she would have written for me.

Udeme Inyang, my literary Queen; a very bold and sincere critic, her company is charged with positive energy, and her enthusiasm for intellectual prowess can drive anyone to heights sublime

Ekaette Umoh, who saw my future as a writer and urged me to write.

Victoria Nkereuwem, my sister, for nagging the life out of me to write, having read my series of short stories that I wrote as a child.

Uduak Favour, my sister and Edidiong Akpaso, my adopted son, for their love and support, charging and keeping my laptop always on point.

My students, both in the secondary and tertiary institutions that I have been privileged to teach for providing the case studies on consequences of good and bad company

Dr Grace David Adewale, my friend and destiny partner, the Lord, used her to give me profound stability at the later end of writing this book. It is easier to start a thing than to finish, but God used her ministry to help me.

Words indeed fail me to rightfully thank Bro Anietie Usen

for his time and concern to see to a proper finish to this book. He stood up for me against the chaos of anti finishing.

My publisher, Azafi Omoluabi, for her team Spirit which endeared me to her person and I could entrust her with my precious book.

I may not remember to mention everyone by name. Still, I cannot forget Pharmacist Ifiok Edede for typing the first manuscript, Ese and Uwakmfon Obonguko for reading the prologue and asking for more.

Thank you is not enough; God bless you all.

CONTENTS

FOREWORD

An old Japanese proverb says, "No road is too long in the company of a good friend." Elizabeth and I have been friends since we were teenagers at the University of Uyo. Our friendship has Journeyed through the years of university, careers, marriages, the birth of our children, and all. It has definitely been a long journey of life, each of us being a witness to the beginning of each chapter of our lives. Yet, ours is a friendship that seems destined to be as we shared so much in common. The trajectory of our lives always crossed, and no matter how far away we were from one another, our paths would always take us to where they struck again.

As teenagers, we loved books; we loved stories. The stories that may seem mundane to others transported us to foreign and exotic lands where imageries in the stories imploded our imagination. We felt every thought and emotion in the characters of the books we read. The stories made us dream, and for Elizabeth, one of those dreams has led to the birth of this first book, "The Return of Judah." Out of her converted heart, her transformed mind, and an authentic relationship with Christ, Elizabeth can tell this story of Judah.

When Elizabeth asked me to write the foreword for this book, it felt daunting. Then I read the book and soon realised that with the Bachelor of Arts degree in English we both earned, I had the necessary foundation to introduce this book. I also have a post-graduate diploma in management, a master's degree in project management, industry-related certifications, and a successful career as a seasoned project manager; leading project teams has given me the skills to be a good storyteller. As you read this, you may wonder what project management has in common with storytelling? Let me make it known that the art of storytelling is essential to being a great leader. From leading teams to coaching to presenting projects to stakeholders and communicating to clients, project success is achieved by telling stories that come from the heart.

Unlike Elizabeth, storytelling does not come naturally to me. Still, drawing from my experiences telling stories of valuable lessons learned while managing projects, I can see how compelling and exciting this story is. The story is so interesting that I could not put it down once I started reading the manuscript. So what is this story about Judah? First, let me tell you what Elizabeth has accomplished. She has artfully woven a simple Bible story of a man who found himself in a lousy company into a beautiful story of redemption, fulfilment of the promise, and purpose of God. That man was Judah, the fourth son of Jacob, who was also called Israel.

"The return of Judah" is unexpectedly daring as the story of Judah and Tamar is often seen as an "ill-favoured story" in the Bible. However, Elizabeth tells this story in a different light. She has said it with "a secular twist," weaving the humanistic attitudes of ordinary people like you and me into a story of hope and redemption that only God can give. In this story, we see ourselves through the eyes and voices of the characters themselves. The way Elizabeth has pulled back and laid bare the hearts of the main characters Judah and Tamar is so skilful that we empathise with them even as they plot evil in their hearts. We also see ourselves in Ingar, whose drunken little slip of the tongue introduces the drama in this story of manipulation, lousy judgment, and family dysfunction.

Indeed I have known this author for over-thirty-something years. However, it is not because of "our company" that I highly recommend this book as a good read. The return of Judah's story is not reminiscent of the story of our friendship nor our company. However, it is a reminder of the truth of Proverbs 27:17 "As iron sharpens iron, so one person sharpens another." In the same manner, a knife that is not sharpened also goes blunt and becomes ineffective. As Elizabeth has been that iron to point me over the years, she has shown in this book that anyone can go dull and lose their purpose in the wrong company.

To so many others, she has also blessed, taught, loved, encouraged, giving of herself, her loyalty, wisdom, and vivacious personality impacting the lives of both young and old. Now she graces us with a skillfully written story about keeping bad company. As you enjoy the drama in this story, this story will also hopefully open up a dialogue with yourself, your company, your place, and your purpose.

Margaret U Thacker, MS, PMP

PROLOGUE

ngar was terrified. He could not believe the strange transformation of the mysterious man before him. His visage had taken on the form of a strange breed, half-man, half-beast as he shouted back at him. Impossible!

She wouldn't dare go a-whoring and defile the family name with her bastard. The hairs on his skin were virtually standing out on his body, and the ones in his nostrils flicked torrentially as he thundered. Such were his fits of anger when his temper was roused. He hardly got angry, but not even a bow of steel would be spared when he did. Judah could eat iron bars with his bare teeth.

Who could stand the feat of such an unearthly display of temper? This was not known to poor Ingar, who found himself at the mercy of the stranger whose favour he had hoped to curry with his juicy tales.

"Bring the infidel here at once," Judah ordered.

She would be put to death for this show of shame. Shelah left his tent at the uproar and hastily ran across the short distance to his father's tent.

"Father, what makes you so upset? I just heard you shouting, and then the fast footfalls of someone I could hardly make out in the distance."

"Your late brother's wife, Tamar, is with child. Obviously, she has been playing the whore, having the pleasures of other men, to the shame and dishonour of this family, Judah answered. I cannot live to take this abomination and disregard he continued; she must die. The law of the land forbids her existence; the land must be purged of her filth. Call the elders and your uncles. Send words to the gate. Let the men prepare the stakes. The young man that brought me the news has gone to tell her father to bring her here. This woman has only brought doom, doom, and more doom, to this family!"

Poor Ingar, he had only expected a few mugs of wine and food from the old widower. How could he have entangled himself in this kind of heinous mess? Tamar was to be burned at the stake! Her insensitive and complacent father would ultimately have to fight for his poor daughter to save her life or give in to her painful and shameful death at the stake, a fitting punishment for her whoredom.

What could he do to extricate himself from this maze of events? Ingar thought as he hurried to find lodging elsewhere. He knew that his life was no longer safe. Whether he took the information to Tamar's family or not, a chain of events had already been set in motion to bring Tamar and her family to book — what with the strong connection between Judah and Hirah. The thought of Hirah brought sweat to his temples.

Hirah was the classic *'Lord of the Flies.'* Athletically built, with a streetwise reputation and his hands in both pastoral and plant cultivation in Adullam and Timnath. he was an influential man who could travel to any part of ancient Canaan and bring friends and strangers to invest in his native land of Adullam. He was a man of the people and was highly respected in the land. The elders held him in high esteem; no one ever toyed with Hirah. Ingar shrank as he sped on to find a place to lay his head as the evening was fast approaching.

Chapter One

THE GLOW OF TAMAR

Tamar smiled to herself at the reflection of her bulge in the mirror. It was a smile of satisfaction and aggrandisement. The God of the Hebrews had finally turned things around in her favour. She gingerly touched her bulging middle and blew a kiss to her unborn child. She was very calm as she imagined what would be the turn of events in the next few days.

She had, on purpose, pushed her stomach to a perspicuous size when she met that drunkard, Ingar, at the spring. Something had come upon her and made her show off her budding pregnancy so that Judah's household would hear of it and react. She could not wait to hear their judgment and spite. Who knows, they might even condemn her to be burnt to death to atone for her sins.

With these thoughts, she turned round to take another look at herself. There was more to her bulge; a beautiful complexion and a glow of victory. All the pains of the past were gone. Who could have believed that her plans would work so perfectly? Her father in-law's hypocrisy of falling for a temple prostitute and parting with his signet, bracelet and staff was unbelievable, hmmm! What the drive of passion could do to a man!

"Oh!" she exclaimed, "Let me see where I kept this treasured evidence of my virtue." She spoke aloud, "There you are! I have the upper hand. At last, I am fulfilled and settled, and Judah would be too incapacitated to do me any harm. I will wait for a few more days; just a few…"

"Tamar! Tamar! Tamar, come out here at once!" her father's voice interrupted her fantasy.

"Father, I am coming," she replied.

She hurriedly hid the objects of Judah's pledge and stepped out to meet the glare of her father.

"What have you done, Tamar? You are with child, and we do not know who the father is? Why have you brought this shame to the family?" Shannon shook his head, apparently confused and at a loss for words. Tamar's mother, Dedan, could be heard sobbing profusely at the corner of the living room. Tamar ran towards her and wrapped her arms around her.

"Mother, it's going to be alright. I did not do anything wrong, believe me."

The mother gazed up at her. "The elders are outside waiting to take you to the stake at the instruction of your father-in-law. It would be best if you had not married the sons of the stranger. Oh, my poor daughter; their ways are different from ours. Judah is determined to purge his house of your defilement by burning you to death. God demands this."

When Tamar heard this, she became conflicted. She wondered if she should tell her parents that it was the same callous man who had put her in the condition or wait until she got to her late husband's residence. While she was still considering the options, her father's voice interrupted her:

"Tamar, you will come later with the elders. Your mother, I and your brothers shall go ahead of you with some other elders of our land to plead your cause. I know that you have been a discreet and virtuous daughter to me. The gods of our fathers will vindicate you. Be calm and speak to no one of the wicked man that has brought this shame upon you."

Tamar became strengthened by her father's words. She quickly ran into her room and retrieved the pledge.

The pledge was a vital determinant in her plan according to the practice of the times; it was an equal exchange given as surety for an agreed price of goods or services. In Tamar's case, she was to be given a kid from Judah's flock of sheep.

Tamar had pretended to be a Prostitute to mislead her father in law to sleep with her to secure her levirate right of raising seed for Er, her late husband, since it was obvious that Judah was not going to give her to Shelah as a wife.

Tamar had deliberately and carefully chosen these objects as they would be undeniable proof that it was Judah who got her pregnant from her late husband's family line. The three objects were distinctively marked as Judah's, because it was only a man of great wealth that could own a Signet which was either in the form of a ring with his symbol to emboss vital documents in his business or a separate Seal for stamping official documents in business transactions. His staff was also marked with his symbol which would directly point him out as the culprit in any case of a denial to secure whatever was pledged for. In all regards, Tamar was confident, that she would topple Judah at his game..

Tamar was also grateful to her childhood friend Deliah whose ingenuity and suggestion birthed this result.

Deliah lived in Betshemesh with her parents, it was rumoured that Reuel; Tamar's elder brother had intentions of courting the maiden but nothing of the sort had happened yet. She was quite fond of Tamar and they shared gossip with each other. She was very sympathetic to Tamar's plight of losing her youthful husband, at the same time, consoling herself over Tamar's peculiar situation of being sent back to her parents as if she was no longer married. The two young women were bonded by their common singlehood. She would visit to help Tamar with her house chores and plait her hair and Tamar would do the same for her.

Tamar recalled one of Deliah's visits a few months ago with news of Shelah's plan to accompany Judah to Timnath; a neighbouring village not quite far from Betshemesh. Deliah had an uncle in Chezib who was close to Judah's family and was privy to his plan to return to work after mourning the loss of his late wife Sheena.

When Deliah informed her at first, it did not occur to her that she could take advantage of the situation to her gain. Her desire was for Shelah, whom she had been interested in, to fill the void of being widowed and alone. She thought to deceive Shelah to lay with him by disguising herself as a harlot to mingle with the prostitutes at Enaim temple of Astarte, the fertility goddess. She had asked questions and studied them with their fanciful dresses and the heavy makeup they used to seduce men. She had to save her money to buy the exotic veils to cover herself from easy recognition. Deliah helped her by lending her some of her jewellery. She also helped to monitor the arrival of Judah's caravan at Timnath.

Tamar could remember vividly the ordeal she passed through that day in order to achieve her desired goal. She had to plan every detail of the deception with precision as it was her last trump card. Although Tamar did not care for the goddess Astarte, she had to make several trips to the temple mound at Enaim to study the layout and rehearse several times so as to not look odd and out of place in the temple. Moreover, the temple's usual crowd of prostitutes had to be familiar with her presence in the inner temple and other areas like the altar of sacrifices so that she would blend with the environment. The most tricky part was knowing the exact day that Judah would arrive since the journey was about three days to the Timnath hinterland where he had his sheepcotes. This made it difficult for her to ascertain the time of his arrival at Enaim, which was a bypass to Timnath. Judah was a Hebrew and only worshipped Astarte to honour his wife. Tamar was not sure that he was still faithful in his temple worship as he was before. This made her jittery, and she had to pray fervently for the help of Yahweh for help in her plight.

She shared her fears with Deliah, who encouraged her by walking with her to the temple every day from the onset of Spring, which set out time for Sheep shearing in Canaan. Sometimes, they would casually stroll on the narrow hilly paths that led to the temple, picking and eating wild fruits as they went. Tamar had to carry the garments to be used for her disguise in a pack hidden inside a jar with either fruits or some figurines to appear as if they were going to worship Astarte. This they did until the day that Deliah sighted the caravan bearing Judah and his friend Hirah. The caravan was obvious because of the peculiar dressing of the Hebrews.

It was a very trying moment as it took sheer bravery for her to adjust her plans when Deliah ran to her from her hideout at the back of the temple surroundings where she was watching from, to warn her that Judah was accompanied only by Hirah. There was no sign of Shelah, only the servants in the caravan belonging to her estranged father-in-law. As soon as Deliah gave her the information, she adjusted her gait and feigned unperturbed, although she was disorganised. Instead, she strolled outside the temple towards the byway. She needed fresh air as she was anxious about the prospect of her success to pull through the deception. However, things moved in her favour as she stood to observe the road only to notice the familiar figure of her father-in-law gliding towards her; she could not believe her luck that Judah was actually walking up to her. When he grinned amorously at her and started asking her name, she sighed with relief, knowing that she was on point. The rest was now history.

As she looked back now, she felt delighted and was ready to face Judah. She tied the signet and the bracelet together, wrapping them around her waist; she decided that the staff would have to be carried in her hand as it could not be concealed in a bag, so she used one of her old veils to cover it, waiting for the moment of her fate. Dedan called from the living room, "Tamar, we are leaving in a short while; your father will come back to escort you to Chezib."

On hearing this, Tamar straightened and heaved a sigh of relief. "It's not so bad; after all, my parents did not press so hard to know the identity of the father of my unborn child. Perhaps, their guilt and passivity towards my plight has impaired them. Who would have believed that my loving father could just watch me metamorphose into a common housemaid in his house, running errands that I never did when I was a child and *single* in this same house!

"My mother completely took advantage of me. She has been most insensitive, using me as a gossip mate to discuss my father, her husband, asking for tips on what to do or what not to do. She has been oblivious to my feelings as a woman and one who has been married twice. The mockery of my siblings, especially Erica, who sends her child home for me to babysit without considering that I am her elder sister… Lord, I cannot wait to get out of this prison, even if I am to go to my den of doom. It is better to be burnt to death with my unborn child than to continue my life in this house of grief."

Chapter Two

THE UNEXPECTED HAPPENS

The four elders — Eglon, Terai, Imvas and Eloys — hurried down to Shannon's house at the beckoning of Reuel, Shannon's son. Shannon came out to meet them. He informed them of his predicament and the evil tidings that the elders of Judah's household had brought concerning his daughter, Tamar.

"We have to move to Hirah, the Hebrew's friend's house. Perhaps he will intervene on our behalf. Let us go to Hirah, our brother; surely, he will speak in our favour."

The elders left immediately for Hirah's house. Hirah, Judah's friend, lived in Adullam. It was a full day's journey to his home. Shannon and the elders would have to move to Adullam and then to Chezib, which was further by another two days. In all, it would take three days to get to Judah's home in Chezib. They needed to see Hirah and beg him to intervene for his daughter. The elders were the jurors in ancient Canaan in the jurisdiction and arbitration of cases of social injustice between its people. Usually, the elders of the families in question would be called upon to the gate (the place of authority; where whatever was agreed became binding or lawful) to sit and deliberate on the matters and arrive at a common verdict before implementing the decision taken. It was late in the night when the team of elders arrived at Adullam but were told that Hirah had already gone to Judah's house. They were left with no choice but to lodge in Adullam for the night and to resume the journey on the morrow to Judah's house to face his wrath.

They quietly left for Judah's house the next day. The journey to Chezib was solemn and mirthless. The elders moved for miles without as much as a word to one other. Apart from the interval stops to give provender and water to the asses they rode, the rest of the journey was in absolute silence. The mood the silence invoked was the feeling Tamar had already been condemned to death. On the third day, since they set off from Betshemesh, they arrived at Chezib. It was already noontime, so they saddled their asses towards the Hebrew's villa. As they got close, Judah's voice could be heard from the distance as he recounted the incident to the men of his house. Judah's voice was quite unusual; it sounded like the rumbling of thunder as he narrated the woes that his daughter-in-law had brought upon his house. The four elders and Tamar's parents were ill at ease as they progressed towards the Hebrew's residence, but courageously, they approached the house knowing that there was no going back.

On beholding them from afar, the enraged Judah screamed, "Where is your shameless daughter, Shannon? She must be tied to the stake and burnt. We will not tolerate such a woman in this house. I sent her to you so that my son Shelah could grow. I did not request a refund of the dowry paid on her behalf. When Er, my first son, died, I gave her to my second son, Onan, and Onan also died. Your daughter has brought me untold hardship since she came into my family. I would have gladly given her to Shelah, my son, if he was not so young, and now, she could not even wait to be given honourably to my son; she had to go into harlotry to reproach me. No! It is enough!" Judah thundered and roared like a lion in want of its prey.

"You are a good man, Judah. You have shown much kindness to our daughter. She is deserving of death for this shame, but please hear us out," the four elders pleaded with Judah. Shelah came between them to restrain his father. At times like this, he wished that his mother, Sheena, was alive to placate him. She was a woman of rare virtue. She could calm the angry sea with her tender gait and demeanour. Sheena was a tiny and soft-spoken woman with exotic looks, a woman whose beauty could melt the heart of any mortal. Judah had been so content with her that he completely forgot the troubles of his father's house. Sheena was a healing balm and an elixir to his turbulent life. He owed her association and friendship to his good friend, Hirah, who came to his rescue as he wandered away from Bethel, far from his father, Jacob.

Shelah pleaded with his father to maintain his calm and show civility to Tamar's parents. Hirah took charge of organising the elders to take them to the gate to attend the proceeding for the hearing, as was the custom. He also admonished his friend to calm down for the necessary protocols to be observed. Judah was adamant as he'd already prepared the stake assuming that Tamar would have no way of escape.

Perhaps he was anxious to get rid of her and spare his son the risk of marrying her and suffer the same fate as his brothers. When the elders were refreshed and were ready for the deliberation, Judah became quiet and pensive; he was anxious to get the verdict over and done with.

After long hours of deliberation, it was agreed that Tamar had trespassed by committing adultery. The penalty was burning. Shannon and his kinsmen tried to reason with the elders that Judah should have given her to his son, who was of age to marry, but it was to no avail. Tamar was to die at the stake. Shannon took his leave immediately to return to Betshemesh to bring his daughter to face her doom. As he left, his wife, Dedan, ran after him wailing and pleading with the elders to show mercy instead of judgment to her daughter.

Chapter Three

A DREADFUL REALITY

Tamar had chosen this moment to dress specially. Decking herself daintily in the same garments she wore on the day she met Judah during the last sheep shearing in Timnath. She graciously carried the little bundle of Judah's pledge and the staff with her. On hearing her mother's familiar wails, she nodded her head, assuring herself that the time she had long awaited was at hand. Shannon was shocked to see his daughter so calm and undisturbed. He was most uncomfortable because she was overdressed, yet he was too confused to question her. Perhaps, he thought, she was trying to make herself happy before her misfortune. He took her hand and held her to himself while he sobbed and heaved, trying to hide his grief as a man.

They had arrived their home the night before. They had spent an extra day at the temple in Enaim to sacrifice in atonement for her sins. They had already told her about the dreadful verdict. To their surprise, Tarmar did not utter a word or gasp to express her grief; she just sighed and tried to soothe her mother, who was worried sick because of her. As they were about to set out for Chezib, a wave of anxiety blew over her, and she gave in and could not maintain her composure anymore. She began to cry and shed the tears that she had withheld all those days of pain, bitterness and denial. She recalled all the abuse, accusations, and the terror of risking sleeping with her father-in-law to alleviate her suffering. Tamar wept, but for a reason other than the fear of death at the stake.

"Father, do not weep for me. It has pleased the Lord to take two men from me, men I married and cared for without any seed. And now, if it pleases Him, let Him take me. I am not afraid. I will go to my husband's people; the God of the Hebrews is a fair judge. He will judge my case and vindicate me."

With these words, Tamar released herself from her father's hold and walked towards the ass that her father had laden with victuals for the journey and mounted it waiting for her father and his accompanying troop to join them to Judah's homestead. When she got to Chezib on the third day, Tamar was a bit anxious, especially for her mother, whose condition had gone worse with the impending doom. Yet, she could not allow the pressure of her mother's grief to make her goof by letting out her secret that there would be a turnaround in her favour. On arrival at Judah's house, her father-in-law's anger was freshly kindled against her. He rose immediately and grabbed her in anger, thrusting her to the men at the stake to tie her. Judah had no consideration for her condition after such a long and tortuous journey. To him, Tamar was as good as dead, but he was in for a big surprise as Tamar shouted out loud, "Let the man whose items these are, discern whether he is the father of my unborn child or not."

When Tamar shouted, Judah was taken aback. When she first entered his house that evening, she looked vaguely familiar, although his anger had blinded any deep interest in her person that he would have had. Now with her scream and boldness to speak after such a grievous accusation, he was afraid. He looked from her to the objects she was displaying for all to see.

Hirah, his friend, was the first to put his head down as he recognised Judah's pledge items. He began to rub the back of his head in shame. On his part, Judah was stupefied beyond words. He froze in his stride when he beheld his signet, bracelet and staff with his name embossed on them. Tamar wrung her hands free from his grip and straightened out, taking a deep breath to hear what her father-in-law had to say to her.

At that point, she wondered what Judah would do to her and the consequences of her outburst. Judah's hands went to his mouth as though to close his accusing lips. He staggered to find a seat for himself.

Meanwhile, the men were waiting eagerly for Hirah's instruction. The whole place was quiet until Judah spoke.

"She is more righteous than I am…" Judah mumbled a justifiable excuse to the teeming bloodthirsty crowd to disperse and not to burn Tamar to death. He explained further, "I refused to give her to Shelah to wife when Shelah had grown."

Tamar turned to her parents and wept. She cried out the pain of injustice, false accusation, condemnation and the woes that befell her as she was exposed in her vulnerability without the covering of a husband. Tamar's parents were only too glad that she was alive, and they did not need any further exchange of words with Judah. He had paid her dowry, and now he had shamelessly admitted to fathering her unborn child. Thank goodness, his wife was dead. In Canaan, there was nothing strange about Judah marrying Tamar himself. With this resolution, Shannon, his wife and the four elders left Judah's house.

Hirah slipped through the crowd and fled like a fiend to his villa. He could not stand the chicken-livered confession of Judah. What did he mean by owning up to a whore like Tamar? Did Judah think that he was the only man that slept with her? The harlot had been openly displaying herself the day they met her, so who knew how many men had had her before Judah came.

He found his friend a coward, not worthy of his alliance andassociTimnath He could not imagine his ever stooping so low as to actually choose Judah as a friend. He was in a foul mood and did not hear his wife, Jezzy, who was curiously waiting to hear the outcome of Judah's next trouble, which he had hurriedly informed her of when he left the house earlier that day.

"How did it go, my lord?" Jezzy inquired from her husband. "Or did it have anything to do with you because you are not clearly in a good mood?"

Hirah tried to ease up a bit by waving her aside with the best of his nonchalant gestures but failed.

Instead, he blurted out, "I thought Judah was a man, but today, right before my eyes, I have seen the kind of coward he is. Can you imagine the gypsy girl he married for his son who died, and when he gave her to raise an heir for the firstborn by the second, that one died also! This girl had the effrontery to conspire and lay in wait for Judah so he would sleep with her while he was on his way to the last sheep shearing at Timnah, which

I had accompanied him to. Jezzy, I was with him; I don't need secondhand information on this; I saw the harlot on the byways at Ena'im, and because we were tired and we needed to stay over for the night, he just wanted to humour himself with female company after his wife had died. This whore was even putting herself out for anyone that cared. Of course, I had no desire for her, so she went to Judah, but today it turns out that it was his daughter-in-law, and she is claiming that Judah is the one who has put her in the family way because the custom demands her death at the stake. Then my so-called friend swallows her claims, hook, line and sinker and instead apologised to the whore, saying that he had wronged her by sending her away and not allowing her to marry his third son and probably kill that one, too."

"Hmmm," Jezzy grunted, "Wonders will never end. So, you mean that the gypsy girl is still alive?"

"Yes!" Hirah screamed emphatically, "She *is* alive, and Judah has taken her in as his wife. It's so revulsive, I can't fathom it. If I wasn't in his company, I would have sworn he was jinxed."

"So, is Judah marrying her to himself or to his third son, seeing that she is with his own pregnancy? This sounds so messy and foolish to me," Jezzy said to her husband.

Hirah sighed impatiently, "You know what? Let's talk about something else. As far as I am concerned, I regret every bit of my time and energy spent with that scoundrel. He does not deserve my association. Find me food to eat, woman, because I am famished!"

It was ironic that just as Hirah the Adullamite had lost taste for his friendship with Judah and felt only spite for him, Judah also felt the same way about him. What might have been that fateful day twenty years ago, when Judah met Hirah and decided to keep company with him? Judah mused. Judah had been carried away by the splendour of his worldly friend Hirah, whose name incidentally meant 'splendour'. With his royalty and wealth in the city of Adullam, Hirah had a free spirit. His parents had been quite liberal with him; he could go wherever he wanted and associate with whomever he chose; his parents were not perturbed. To them, a man was free to do as he pleased and did not need rules and restrictions.

Because Judah's parents used to impose their wills upon him, Judah was hungry for adventure. He felt like he needed to live his own life on his terms; he had come of age to choose for himself, and so with a friend like Hirah who had the kind of parents he did, Judah had a welcome party waiting to receive him. Hirah influenced Judah in several ways: in his beliefs and values, his tastes and cravings. Judah was completely carried away by his new environment in Adullam, the hustle and bustle of city life, with its compensating conveniences and advancements. Judah was utterly drawn to the 'affluence' that this friendship offered him. He did not have to go to worship his father's God with him anymore, something he was glad about because those blessings of the Shabbat that his father used to pronounce on them every Friday had become boring and monotonous to him. The women in Adullam were fashionable and exotic compared to the dull Hebrew maidens in their settlement at Edar.

Hirah was not just a friend but an enigma, the negative instrument planted on his path to stop Judah and nip him in the bud of destiny, although in absolute subtlety. God had promised

Abraham that the Redeemer of mankind would come through his descendant. Hirah was an instrument and agent of Satan positioned in Judah's life to mar his vision, corrupt his desire and blind his discernment in order to severe his chances in the ancestry of the Messiah. This unholy alliance and its influence could never have been known to him. He was just living his life unaware of the schemes of destiny he was powerless to control — except by his choices.

Unfortunately, Judah's life is a reminder to young people to have and cultivate good friendships and company with like minds in order to avoid the corruption and subtlety that the world outside the true God holds. Hirah was a mocker to Judah's destiny.

Although he seemed to have succeeded long enough, yet when he least expected it, Judah mustered the courage to make the first move which culminated in the subsequent strides that led him back to the path of righteousness and God. Hirah, on the other hand, was disappointed and furious. He knew that his aim had been defeated, and friendship with Judah would leave little or nothing to be desired anymore.

Although Judah seemed to be in a mess at the moment, Hirah could predict that the consequences of his admittance would save Tamar's life and ultimately that of the baby in her womb, bringing joy at the time of her delivery. Hirah was so insightful that he would think and scheme ahead on the impact of his word and actions on the people he came in contact with, depending on what his desired objective was. Hirah was the devil's advocate. In this case, he had lost and would await another convenient time. It all depended on Judah.

Chapter Four

DAYBREAK

Judah was running in a large field towards his brothers. He counted them, eleven in number. He shouted their names: "Reuben, Simeon, Levi, Issachar, Zebulun, Dan, Asher, Gad, Joseph, Benjamin and Naphtali." Then he awoke.

"Joseph? Why? Joseph; he is dead. Joseph is no more. He could not have survived in the hands of the Ismaelites, such a spoilt and tender lad. I have not been much of a dreamer like him," Judah thought. "How could I see him in my dream running with the others?"

This dream puzzled Judah. He had earlier succumbed to a drunken sleep after pleading with Tamar to forgive him and assuring her that he would not touch her or make any further unlawful demands on her. He had also assigned his servants to clean an apartment and be at her beck and call. He went out of his way to make sure that he added extra comfort for her, hoping to make up for the abuse she had suffered in his hands. Having satisfied his remorseful mind, he had drunk himself to sleep.

For the first time since his sojourn in Canaan, he was nostalgic; he missed his brethren and his father's house. Judah pondered deep into the night, and he began to consider the life he was now living compared to the standard that his father had set for them back in Edar. He remembered his childhood when he was free and incapable of weighing his actions and inactions, his father's devotion to the God of Isaac, his grandfather, and Abraham, his great grandfather. His father's stories about the God that visited him on his flight to Paddan-aram and made a covenant to protect him in his journeys. He also recalled his father's zeal to run to Bethel for refuge when Simeon, himself and Levi killed the men of Shechem. He longed to have that kind of trust and surety in God now.

Judah's thoughts ran deep to the last time he saw Joseph, his father's favourite son. He realised that he could have done more to save the boy's life that day at Dotham, yet they suggested that he should be sold. He remembered the agony of his father when they conspired and lied that Joesph had been killed by a wild beast. Judah's conscience plagued him. It was this same guilt-ridden conscience that had made his stay in his father's house unbearable. The incidents came clearly and vividly to him as he remembered packing a few clothes and heading towards Canaan. He recalled his stop at the Inn that night to rest and his first encounter with Hirah. Hirah the Adullamite was a jolly good fellow, coming to his rescue with his cowboy gait and generous spirit. He spotted Judah in the corner where he had hidden to eat his first meal of the day. He was dog-tired from his long walk through the back ways to Adullam. Hirah walked up to him and shook hands, asking what a Hebrew lad like him was doing in their territory. Judah feared that the question could bring further troubles if he did not think fast enough and give a tangible reason for straying into the ungodly neighbourhood.

"Your maidens are lovelier than ours," he replied with his best lustful smile. To this, the shrewd Hirah winked with a mischievous grin to assent his understanding. It was not long before the two got along as if they had known each other from childhood. Judah expressed his desire to stay in Chezib and to marry a Canaanite damsel eventually. Hirah assessed Judah and found that there was no guile in him. Hirah was content to invite Judah to his lodge. Judah was only too delighted to go with this stranger willing to take him in and give him the opportunity for a fresh start in Canaan.

Hirah was from Adullam, the capital of Canaan, so this pleased the adventurous Judah as he looked forward to living in a town instead of the remote settlement where his father Jacob dwelt. Hirah took Judah to his lodge, and there Judah met his future father-in-law, Shuah. The Canaanite had a beautiful daughter, Sheena, and it was not long before Judah's eye caught the attention of Sheena.

Hirah advised Judah to either marry her to avoid trouble with Shuah or steer clear of any inordinate involvement with her as such could bring disharmony between them.

With this wise counsel, Judah boldly approached Shuah for Sheena's hand in marriage. Shuah was glad to oblige Judah as he had a lot of respect for Hirah, his kinsman. Sheena was a very fruitful woman and gave Judah three healthy sons in quick succession. Er was Judah's first, followed by Onan and Shelah the last born. With the birth of his sons, Judah was welcomed and fully accepted in Adullam. When his family enlarged, he moved away from Shuah to live in Chezib. Had his father not told them that God had promised their great grandfather, Abraham, that He would give the land of Canaan to him for an inheritance? Judah, therefore, beat his chest in contentment and relaxed in the land of Chezib.

He soon acquired landed property and was involved in all the socio-cultural and economic activities of the land. He also worshipped Astarte, the Canaanite goddess, and his good friend, Hirah, became an indispensable companion who Judah looked up to for counsel and directives whenever he had challenges. He soon forgot the sorrows and troubles of his father's house.

When the firstborn son of Judah was about fifteen years of age, Judah took for him a wife, Tamar, a maiden from Betshemesh. Er was not as fortunate as his father and died shortly after marriage. This turn of events shook Judah because he was looking forward to becoming a grandfather. After his mourning and the burial of his first son, Judah gave Tamar to his second son, Onan, to raise seed for his late son, Er. This was the practice of the times, but Onan refused to raise seed for his late brother and instead chose to spill his semen each time he met with Tamar. This displeased God, and Onan also died.

Judah was no longer at ease in his newfound haven. The death of his second son and with no sight of an heir from any of his sons left Judah in a very pensive state. Sheena's poor health, borne out of grief for her sons, did not leave much to make his life desirable. Judah was melancholic; he saw himself in a vicious cycle, and for the first time in his eighteen years of dwelling in Chezib, he felt homesick and longed for his father's house.

Then Sheena died. This was the greatest of his grief. His tender loving wife, the reason for his stay in Chezib, had ebbed out of his grip. Perhaps he was wrong to have left his mother. Judah hardly ever thought about his mother or his only sister, Dinah. He was so self-centred in his quest for a better life. He wept, but his weeping was to no avail. He mourned for Sheena longer than was necessary — he was always found in mourning clothes sitting with his hands on his chin and a faraway look in his eyes, seeming to perpetually wonder if it was true that his wife was no more.

Chapter Five

THE LURE OF SPLENDOUR

Shelah, Judah's only surviving son, had grown into a sturdy young man of about seventeen. He was in every sense a man; he had already grown a beard and was conscious of stares from maidens in the temple as they went to sacrifice to Astarte. It was time for the sheep shearing of his father's sheep in Timnath, and there was excitement in the city as men and women prepared for the exercise.

The Sheep Shearing festival was always a special and remarkable feast in the South East. It was celebrated in early spring, sandwiched between the grain or cereal harvest and the in gathering harvest of fruits in Canaan. It was a period of reunion as many Strangers and relatives outside Canaan visited at this time to unite and rejoice with their loved ones. It was also a time to settle disputes and pay homage to God in appreciation for his provision of both food and clothing. The sheep were selected according to the amount of wool on their body. If the animal was not ready for shearing, it could endanger its life as the change of season may affect the sheep's health. In those days, certain people who has skills in shearing were hired for the work. The wool sheared from the various sheep cotes would be dyed and separated from others for easy identification. Sheep shearing was a good source of income generation in the Southeast.

Shelah looked forward to this event, as he was hoping to go with his father to help, and he hoped to also discuss his personal affairs with him. His mother's death and the previous deaths of his elder brothers had brought a shadow of darkness and pain over their household. There had been a growing distance between him and his father as each clung to his grief. Fortunately, his father's good friend Hirah had returned from his trip to the North and visited his father to console him over Sheena's demise. This particular visitor was able to break the norm of Judah's grief and cause him to shed his mourning clothes and wash after long days of grieving.

Shelah was fantasising about the possibility of either choosing his bride or waiting for Tamar who had been sent back to her parents pending his maturing. He had looked forward to marrying Tamar, whom he found very attractive even in his childlike eyes. He remembered her kindness and sweet tenderness towards him when she was with his brothers.

Tamar was adorable and very submissive, unlike the other maidens he had encountered. He did not want to displease his father in any way by going against his will in his marriage. Yet, he had to talk things through with Judah as they would be going to Timnath. Perhaps, since Timnath was just a few miles from Betshemesh, they might send for Tamar to join them. Shelah was startled from his reverie when Judah entered his room. He had decked himself with a bright new cassock and an exotic turban. He was carrying his signet and staff, obviously set to leave for Timnath. "Son, I will be leaving for the sheep shearing." Shelah started, "But father, I was hoping to go with you, have a change of scene, and talk. I mean, it's been a while…" Judah shook his head and said, "Another time, Shelah. You don't want to keep your uncle Hirah waiting." And with that, Judah left for Timnath.

It was fun to be with Hirah again, travelling on the plains of Chezib to the cities of the outskirts where the sheep shearing would be taking place. Judah felt refreshed from the breath of the fresh country air; it had been ages since he had enjoyed the luxury of mounting a horse and smelling the wind again. He was grateful to his friend, whom he owed a lot. Hirah was responsible for his many fortunes in the land of Canaan; his house in Chezib, the sheepcotes at Timnath and even his marriage.

Owning several sheepcotes in those days was an indication of great wealth. A sheepcote is a small hut where sheep, lambs and goats are kept to be tended by shepherds. It was a very lucrative business in Canaan at the time, and wealthy merchants could own several sheepcotes — depending on how large the animal farm was. There were cotes for cattle such as donkeys, asses and camels. Judah was also rich in cash crops, like raisins, pomegranates and pears. He also planted a large vineyard in Canaan.

As they rode, Hirah teased him about his cowardice in mourning for a woman for so long, when he could have married immediately after his mourning days were fulfilled. He made suggestions on how Judah could travel with him to Jerusalem, the land of the Jebus, to see the exotic maidens there, but Judah declined. It was getting to sunset, and they were tired, so they decided to stopover at Enaim where there would be lodging as it was a bustling settlement because of the temple at that location.

As they turned towards their lodging, between the bypass of Enaim and Betshemesh, Hirah sighted a gaily dressed woman standing on the way; he beckoned to Judah and gave him a wink. Now, Judah had not had the pleasure of a woman in a long while since he was in mourning for a long time after the death of his wife and Hirah's teasing was not helping him. Rather, they were stirring amorous desires in him even more. He looked at Hirah and then at the harlot as though seeking Hirah's consent in this instance, Judah disembarked and turned to the harlot, feeling a strange excitement of achievement. The feeling of not being an underdog was always surfacing whenever Hirah the Adullamite dared him. The man was capable of making him do the unimaginable and unthinkable. Hirah was his cheerleader and had the ability to evoke the male chauvinistic tendencies in him that were passive due to his religious values and upbringing.

Judah addressed the strange woman, and without much ceremony, he told her that he wanted her company for the rest of the day. To this, the harlot willingly agreed and stated her price. Not being a dubious man, Judah told her that he did not carry cash about, but he had to stop over to court her because he could not resist her beauty. His statement was flattering to the lady, but she had a more pressing need to secure her price, and she did that by asking him to give a surety for his pledge to pay her at a later date. Judah obliged and saddled the lady on his horse to his lodge for the evening.

Unknown to Judah, Tamar, his daughter-in-law, had heard that he was coming to his sheepshearers in Timnath. Judah kept reliving the day of his woe as though he could do anything to change what had happened, but it was all to no avail. The incident had taken place four months ago, and now, he was expecting a child from his daughter-in-law. He shook his head and got up to walk around his bed-chamber, an act that did not help his foul disposition.

Chapter Six

ERICA

At Ena'im, news of Judah and Tamar's affair was spreading like wildfire. Erica's husband, Carmi, was uncomfortable with what he had just heard at the Inn. He could not wrap his head around the news of Tamar's close shave with death. He lost the desire to sit with his friends as he usually did on such evenings. He had to hurry home to tell his wife, Erica, Tamar's sister. He wondered why his wife's parents or any of her brothers did not consider informing them of Tamar's plight. As he neared his home, he had second thoughts about telling Erica the news. Rather, he decided to wait to probe her about Tamar and observe his wife's countenance so he could determine if they had deliberately kept the matter from him.

Erica welcomed him home and was surprised because he would usually spend quality time at the Inn and return home late.

"What is wrong, Carmi? Are you ill, or has any of your friends upset you?" she asked.

"None of those reasons, Erica. I just did not feel up to it anymore tonight, so I decided to come home. Or don't I have the right to change my mind and come home to my beautiful wife?" he asked her playfully. During the small talk, he casually asked, "Have you been to see Tamar today?"

"No," Erica quickly replied, "She has been making faces lately, and I guess she's jealous, and so I decided to ease up a bit. I mean, I know she misses her husband and is sad about not having a child of her own. I see the way she looks at Joella when she tends her…"

As Erica spoke, her husband watched her intently and became convinced that she had no idea about what had happened to Tamar.

He cleared his throat and told her, "My dear, Tamar missed death narrowly a few days ago. I heard from my friends at the Inn that her father-in-law heard that she was with child and was so angry at the news, claiming that she had played the whore. So, he summoned your parents and ordered them to bring Tamar to the stake to face the penalty that her offence required. Ironically, when Tamar got to her father-in-law's house, she presented the pledge her father-in-law had given, presuming she was a harlot and had had the pleasure of intimacy with her, not knowing she was his daughter-in-law. Tamar announced to her accusers that Judah, her father-in-law, was the father of her unborn child. This gave the men pause, and Judah admitted that she was right and was a better person than him, who had refused to give her to his last son, Shelah, who was of age to marry.

Erica was rooted to her seat, not knowing whether to cry or laugh. She was too shocked for words as her husband recounted the sordid details of Judah and Tamar's affair. When Carmi was done speaking, she stood up and said calmly to him, "Please take me to my father's house; I want to see my family."

Her husband discouraged the idea because it was already late that day and promised to take her there first thing the following day. The next morning, before the sun was up, Erica had already had a bath and made Joella ready, and without even waiting for Carmi to wake up, she was on her way to her father's house. She was so engrossed in her thoughts and could hardly notice or recognise the people that she was passing on the way. As she neared her home settlement, she sensed someone staring at her and turned impulsively, only to realise that it was Ingar, their childhood friend. She expected him to smile and greet her in his half-drunken way as he usually did, but he was different this time. He acted as if he had just seen a ghost. Erica could not ignore him, so she asked, "Where are you going this morning, Ingar? Is it not too early to go for a drink? Did you hear what happened to Tamar and how Astarte saved her from the Hebrew? Why did you not come to tell me?"

Ingar listened, first with guilt and then relief as the reality of what Erica said dawned on him. "So, Tamar is alive," he thought aloud.

"Yes," Erica answered. "So you did not hear, Ingar? Well, God has vindicated her and today she is not only free but will soon be a mother, which is something she wanted the most."

Ingar could not believe what he was hearing; that Judah, the old widower who had mourned his late wife as if she was the only woman on earth, could still have the pleasure of a harlot. A harlot, who happened to be his daughter-in-law, and then when he heard that she was pregnant, he was so angry to the point of wanting her dead.

"What a world," Ingar thought, as he recalled Judah's fit of anger when he gave him the information, though he dared not divulge his involvement in the matter to Erica. While Erica turned to her father's house in excitement, wanting to get the full details of her sister's escapade, Ingar took a bold step forward as a free man.

The guilt of his tale-bearing had imprisoned him for days, but today, his fate had changed by the good news he had just heard from Erica. He could now face the world again, and he would learn to mind his own business from then on. He had learnt a few lessons. Moreover, he had overcome his drinking habit as the nightmares of Tamar's death kept him awake most nights after his encounter with Judah. If he had not gone to get a few mugs of wine, there would have been no need to go to the old widower in the first place. Looking back at the incident, Ingar was still ashamed of the role he had played in the whole matter and pledged to himself that he would have to apologise to Tamar the next time he met with her.

Chapter Seven

TAMAR'S DREAM

Tamar slept deeply and peacefully. She dreamt of her unborn babies toddling towards her as if they were born already. One of them was a carbon copy of Er, and the other looked like his grandfather, or rather his father, Judah. It was intriguing that the child she was expecting had become two inside her. She made to look at her protruding middle, and then she awoke.

"Oh, it was a dream," she sighed in relief. Could she be carrying twins? She pondered. She then resolved that it was all well, so she would have double for her trouble.

Tamar yawned as she became aware of the familiar surroundings, her home that Judah had deprived her of all these years. She could not deny her gratitude to the God of Abraham, that Judah used to tell her husband, Er, about, although Er did not believe his father's strange tales of the unknown God. Tamar believed those stories and desired in her secret heart to meet this God. More so, when she lost her first and second husbands, it was to this God that Tamar cried to. Her faith in the God of the

Hebrews had paid off finally. When she planned to trick Judah, she had pleaded with this God to help her conceive, knowing that her God Astarte had denied her sacrifices at the temple by striking her two husbands dead and finally abandoned her by causing Judah to send her back to her parents. Tamar also realised that she had lost her home when Shelah grew up, and Judah made no effort to send for her. It was then that she directed her petitions to the unknown God. Now her desires had come to fruition; she would be a mother, and going by the last dream she had, she would be a mother of twins, twin boys!

Tamar was elated. She could not believe the twist of fate. She stretched her legs that were already aching from the tension of the previous day. She basked in the absolute pleasure of the luxury of lying down without having to run errands for her mother. She remembered how terrified she had been when she first discovered her pregnancy and how she had to hide her nauseous state to cope with the house chores.

"Thank God," she exhaled, "All that is history now." Tamar could not stop herself from reminiscing on the invisible hand of grace in her circumstances. She wished that she could sing out her gratitude to Yahweh, as the Hebrews called the unknown God.

How could she forget how diligent she was with her husband? Er, and their youthfulness which should have guaranteed early procreation. But it was not to be. Er died of no known cause; he had not even been feverish, leaving her childless and unfulfilled. The ordeal of coping with his not too pleasant brother, Onan (who was as queer as his name), just to hold forth her hope of having children to comfort her in her grief was to no avail. Yet in just one fleeting moment of obscure pleasure, as she considered it, she conceived. Indeed children are a reward from God; man has no part in it. This was Tamar's conclusion. She resolved that she would serve Yahweh and tell her sons about this God who answered her and saved her when even her parents forsook her.

Chapter Eight

SHELAH LEAVES CHEZIB

Shelah saw Tamar through the window of his room. She was looking so radiant and beautiful in her pregnancy that it took a lot of restraint to keep him from thinking about her as his wife. He hoped that things had turned out the way he had dreamed before the sheep shearing. Perhaps they would have been married by now, and the child she was carrying would have been his. But the way fate played itself out on the affairs of his family made him completely confused. He thought about his father and what the turn of events had done to his manly pride. He felt very sorry for Judah to be entangled in such a position to publicly admit his shame. But he was also out of wits on how to face the old man. Was this his 'secret' desire to deny him his right as a husband to Tamar and then turn around to take her himself? The mere thought of it made him sick. Moreover, it annoyed him that his father expected him, Shelah, to stick with him and play the saintly role of nursing him and his stupid ego by living with Tamar in the same house.

The death of his mother bit Shelah really hard this time, and he wished he had someone to vent his battered soul to. How would he face Judah now, or rather, how would his father face him?

What could he possibly say to exonerate himself? There were so many questions on Shelah's mind. He needed to step outside the house and perhaps not return. Shelah quickly packed his bag. He did not need to carry much clothing since he wanted to appear as casual as possible to avoid attracting the attention of any of the servants. As the sunset approached Canaan, Shelah left Chezib for good.

Unknown to Shelah, Judah saw him leave the house with his backpack. He knew from the set expression on his face that he would not be coming back home that night or ever. Shelah was leaving him for good; what could he do to stop him? The familiar world of a closely knitted family he had once known eluded him. First, his son Er, then Onan, then his dear wife Sheena, and now Shelah: all gone. He was stuck with himself if, indeed, there was anything left of him.

Where did he go wrong? Why was life so unfair? He thought he had it all under control when he settled in Chezib, far away from his father and his own troubles. He thought about Hirah, his friend, and realised that his friend had left immediately after his confession of guilt to Tamar. He could not even wait to help him in that trying moment. He felt a raw sense of resentment towards Hirah. How could he just abandon him now? In fact, it was as if his eyes were opened for the first time so that he saw that this so-called friend of his was always leading him into one straitjacket situation or the other.

What he had considered as "blessings" a few years back now looked like deathtraps to him. Everything that he thought he had achieved had just eclipsed, and worse of all, his image was also gone with it. Chezib, Hirah, and the land he had acquired had all lost their lustre to him.

He did not see Tamar until she coughed and genuflected before him in greeting. Judah mumbled his answer, "I hope you are comfortable and in good health, my daughter?" He managed to speak as calmly as possible. "I am alright, father, and I want to thank you for your generosity." At this comment, Judah became expressionless, not knowing what to say or how to react. Tamar went on as if she was not sure of what to say. "I have looked everywhere for Shelah, but he is nowhere to be found. None of the servants seems to know his whereabouts. Would you know where he is? The house is quite solitary and strange from what it used to be."

Judah motioned to her to sit. It seemed that she was asking for too much, but all the same, he would have to explain things in the best way he could to her.

"When I refused to give you to Shelah in marriage as I had promised, it was not you alone I wronged. I had also wronged and hurt my son. I did not dare to tell him to marry another woman when you were rightfully his, according to our custom. I was also afraid that the plight of his brothers would befall him. He also gladly bore with me until…" his voice broke.

Tamar could not hold herself any longer. She went to him and took his hands, telling him to say no more as she understood his position. Judah continued, "Shelah has left me without even saying a word. He considers me treacherous, and that justly so."

There was an awkward silence after this brief exchange of words. She did not know what to say, so she made up an excuse to leave and retired to her room. Everything was so out of place; the house was cold with no one to talk to except the strange and distant servants who probably could not wait to go to their quarters with their firsthand tales of her predicament. She missed her mother-in-law, Sheena. Tamar wished that Judah's wife was still alive, and although the present situation would have stirred up jealousy and probably spite, yet as a woman, she would have understood and empathised with her condition.

Chapter Nine

TAMAR'S LONELINESS

Tamar had the strangest of feelings; she was listless and uncomfortable. She couldn't explain exactly how she felt; then, she discovered to her chagrin that she needed male company and affection. She craved the warmth and comfort of a man as she remembered Er in the familiar environment. Self-loathing and regrets enveloped her for throwing herself at her father-in-law without considering the consequences. While she was with her parents, she did not seem to experience any of these feelings. Still, it seemed that as soon as the tension over her vengefulness was resolved, her system had taken on the reality of the peculiar needs of a pregnant woman. This was strange, and she did not bargain for it at all. She wished it was possible for her to go back home to confide in her mother and seek her elderly counsel, but that would be out of place, considering her circumstance.

She went to Judah out of sheer frustration for lack of one to talk to. It would have given her a sort of relief if she had met Shelah, who was a younger person, to at least make some idle conversation with, but unfortunately, it was not to be. The frankness of Judah was rather irritating to her initially since she considered that he was directly responsible for the boomerang of misfortune that had befallen the family. Yet, despite her misgivings, she thought it wise to keep her feelings under check as Judah had made it clear that he would not compromise any form of affection between them any further. She would have to bear her inconveniences until her time of delivery.

The thoughts of her vulnerability brought tears to her eyes. She was very conflicted because there was no one with whom she could share her thoughts and fears. She also missed her mother, who seemed so far away from her now. Although she made friends easily, she could not bring herself to confide in Anna, her nurse. The only confidant she could have would be Yahweh, whom she spoke aloud to when no one was around. She told all her fears and cravings to Yahweh. For lack of an activity to engage in, Tamar decided to pick the weeds competing with the goodly vegetables in the garden.

From all indications, the garden was just thriving on previous care, and it was evident that it had not been tended for a long time. But for the drought, the weeds would have completely taken over. When she realised the poor state of some of the vegetables, Tamar decided to go to the house to get the shears and pruning hooks so she could trim the dead edges off the wild creepers. She also realised that the work was good exercise for her as she had not done any form of house chores or outdoor tasks since she came to Judah's house.

As she worked, she occupied her mind with thoughts of her

unborn child or children. She really wanted to have a son, one that would grow into a man, keep her company and protect her when he was grown. She had decided that she would not marry any man after her previous ordeal; instead, she would care for her son and be a good mother and grandmother to her son's children when he married his own wife and had a family.

Tamar looked forward to her delivery and when her status would change to that of a mother. She fantasised about the safe arrival of the baby and the joy that the birth would bring to the family.

The lonely days would also be forgotten, and once more, the house would be full of friends and relatives who would come to welcome the new baby. Moreover, if she delivered twins, Judah would be consoled of the demise of his two sons.

Many scenarios ran through her head as she worked with the shears, and she was so occupied that she did not realise she had spent the whole morning in the garden until it was well after the lunch hour. When Anna called her name, she was jolted from her thoughts, and when she observed her shadow, she was able to tell that the time was far past noon. Anna must have returned with lunch for her and to make her routine check for the day. On hearing her name, she quickly shouted back, "Coming!" and picking up the tools; she hurried back to her room. Anna was perplexed to see her carrying the implements to the store before coming to greet her.

"Why did you stress yourself so, Tamar? You should not do that again. You need to pamper yourself at the time, and except for the walks, you do not need to involve yourself in any strenuous activity."

Tamar merely smiled at Anna and said, "My mother does a lot of work from early to late pregnancy, and you say my simple act of pruning vegetables is strenuous? I am bored, Anna. I was already used to working and not sitting and sleeping all day as I seem to do these days. I need to occupy myself one way or the other."

Anna shook her head as she could relate to her boredom. "Well, surely you would need a warm bath and some stretching, so you can relax," Anna said.

"Thank you for your concern. But I will be just fine," Tamar retorted and walked into her room. Tamar ate well. She had a healthy appetite. The exercise and venting of her thoughts to Yahweh had been good for her. She finished her food, and after the warm bath that Anna fixed for her, she slept.

Chapter Ten

SELF REALISATION

Judah felt hungry for the first time in days. It was four days after Tamar's return to the villa. His hunger was a strange but welcome feeling. He had lacked the luxury of an appetite ever since the series of events that led to his confession to Tamar. He wandered into the private dining room he had shared with his late wife and found some *challa* which the maid had kept for him. He could not tell how long the delicacy had been there but bit into the tender egg ball in abject abandon. There was wine on the table as well, and he gulped down the wine and helped himself generously to the *matzo,* chewing at the chicken lumps as he munched.

Unknown to him, the maid had been picking the untouched meals and kept replacing them with different delicacies to tempt his appetite. Noadia, his maid, was a gracious woman who had absolute loyalty to Sheena, her late mistress. She had lived with Sheena's mother until her demise before transferring her services to Judah and Sheena. She loved the family and served them as she would serve her own children. She was middle-aged but still very strong. Although she had no way of meddling in Judah's private affairs, she felt so much pity for Judah, who she believed was a good man whom circumstances had only pushed to go astray.

Noadia decided that the most she could do to help poor Judah would be to prepare many of her tempting recipes to help him recover from his self-hate.

Judah felt alive again. He could not believe the peace and tranquillity that came over him. He searched within himself for what the source of his peace could be, but he could not pinpoint it. Only a few days ago, he had been swallowed up by anger, followed by shame and the rejection of his only son, Shelah. Then Tamar's inquisition of Shelah's whereabouts triggered him out of his death trap to give an explanation to her. Amazingly, he staggered forth to admit his fault by telling Tamar that he had not wronged only her but his son also.

How uncertain he was, at the time he spoke, of the effects that his few words carried. First, Tamar was affected enough to pity him to the point of actually taking hold of his hands, and as a daughter would her father, she comforted him. Her touch and reaction did not insinuate lust, nor did it remind him of his incestuous error. On his part, he received the warmth of her touch and words as a ready balm to his burning soul. He felt forgiven by her even though she made no mention of the feud between them.

No more did Judah feel guilty. He had released himself, and his conscience was free. His son was justified to abandon him. To Judah, a new journey had begun; self-examination, inward searches and consideration of others, their actions or inactions. A series of deliberate intentions that culminated in absolute social harmony was in order. Little wonder his old father, Jacob, used to be so accommodating after making peace with God and his brother Esau. Judah thought deeply.

As he ate, he began to think more about his father and the stories that he had told his children about the Jewish God, Yahweh.

Yahweh was the God of truth and judgment. Judah recalled his father's blame on Simeon and Levi over their cruelty in Shechem. Unlike his early life, when he was used to struggling and fighting his twin brother Esau and always having the upper hand, Israel had changed. In fact, he had been changed from within by Yahweh. Truly his person as Israel was quite different from who he had been as Jacob. Their father was now calm and reticent. He hardly lost his temper over any issue.

Judah and his brothers had all been taken aback when he did nothing about Dinah's defilement but rather blamed his brothers, who undertook the charge to avenge their sister. Initially, they had thought that Israel was weak and queer. Judah and his brothers were also left in wonder about how he believed them when they lied to him about the death of Joseph. Truth be told, it was his lack of rage and his inward grief that perturbed his sons more than any supposed outburst they had expected. Israel believed them and probably accepted his fate, seeing Joseph's 'death' as one of his portion of mishaps to build his faith more in God. This began to give Judah a new and glaring awareness that there were deep things that his father could have been pondering on, as he was currently doing now, which made him the person that he had become.

Chapter Eleven

REMINISCENCES

After eating till he was full, Judah had a warm bath and continued to take his mind back to his childhood days to find answers to the issues that he had overlooked before. He remembered his mother, Leah. Once, she had told him that his name, *'Yehudah'* in the Hebrew tongue, meant *'praise'*. She had told him that in giving birth to a fourth son, she owed Yahweh incredible praise for lifting her head despite the favouritism of Jacob. His mother had directed her faith towards God, and in Him, she had had the upper hand in her marriage. Rachel had died at childbirth, and now the stiff competition for his mother's place was over.

Judah's thoughts about Yahweh and His ways stirred up questions in his mind. He longed to share his feelings with someone, but the question was, with whom? Hirah did not appeal to him in that regard anymore, and besides, he would not have answered since he was an alien to the ways of the Hebrews. He would go to Israel, his father. At the thought of his father, Judah winced. He had left the old man at a time of grief, while he was still sore from the pain of Josephs's supposed death. He had not even stopped by to see his father over the years because Jacob had disapproved of his Canaanite wife, Bathshuah, as Sheena was called in the Hebrew tongue.

Now, by a twist of fate, he had become a man of many sorrows, having lost his sons and wife in quick succession.

To worsen it all, he now had a dent on his person from his escapade with Tamar. When he considered the different arrows of trouble, shot at him, he remembered his father's tales in Paddan-aram, and he knew within him that his father would provide the answers to the nagging questions that plagued his soul.

Judah called his eldest servant, Machir, and instructed him to take charge of the household affairs and direct the maid to take special care of Tamar. He left sufficient provision for their use and left for his father's habitation in Edar.

Machir called out to Anna. She was the nurse that Judah had assigned to Tamar to attend to her daily and act in the capacity of a companion to her so that Tamar would not need to seek his attention as he was not able to give her any.

Anna was a very understanding lady and a very efficient midwife, well-known for her skills in tending to pregnant women until they delivered safely. She was glad to be called upon to serve in the villa because Judah was popular as a wealthy merchant in Chezib.

She also considered it an honour for her to be of service to the old widower, knowing that she would enjoy many fringe benefits.

Moreover, she was single, and did not mind being a companion to Tamar, who was only slightly younger.

Anna had to move into the villa to ensure that she carried out all her duties efficiently and she was ready at all times to be with Tamar. When Machir informed her that their master had gone on a journey to an undisclosed destination, Anna grimaced in disappointment as if she had missed the opportunity to discuss Tamar's affairs with him. Machir interrupted her thoughts, saying that the master had left sufficient money should there be an emergency and that food and provisions had been adequately made for them. So, except for Judah's physical presence, everything would run smoothly in the villa.

"How is Tamar?" Machir went on to enquire from Anna.

"She is alright and coping with her condition. She is a smart and strong young woman. Her gods have remembered her husband Er at last. She will bear a child for her late husband; God bless his soul."

As if on cue, Tamar came out of the room and gingerly strolled towards Anna.

"Good morning," she muttered to both Machir and Anna. She was always ill at ease with Judah's servant, what with the way he would run his eyes over her. She beckoned to Anna to come to her. Anna moved quickly to her.

"How are you feeling, Tamar? Are you alright?"

"Yes. Only, I feel some movements; a lot of it, actually. The movements are strange and make me rather uncomfortable."

"You should not be; it is normal. Your baby is healthy and strong; that is why it is kicking. I would love to have a look at you. Let's go inside."

In the bedroom, the nurse made Tamar lie down, and after

palpating her, she pondered for a moment before asking her whether she had twins in her family. The nurse made her sit up while she interviewed her further.

"How would you feel if you give birth to two babies instead of one?"

At this, Tamar smiled and, stroking her bulge, said, "I would not be surprised because I had a dream and I saw two babies, not one.

I have been puzzled ever since. I would thank Yahweh for His mercies in giving me double for my trouble."

Anna fixed Tamar's bath, and after helping her dress and change her beddings; she left Tamar for the day.

When Anna was gone, Tamar decided to take a walk to the vegetable garden that her mother-in-law had planted behind the villa. She had longed for something to chew to control her nauseous state and the succulent looking lettuce and cucumber generously sprouting everywhere in the garden were so inviting. She plucked at the vegetables and savoured their tender goodness. As she munched, she could not help but muse at the possibility of her prospective twin birth.

"Could this be true?" To think that just a few months ago, she was a hopeless and abandoned widow, but by an uncanny turn of circumstances, she was now acclaimed to be not just an expectant mother but expecting two babies. How could God be so generous to her, a miserable harlot? She knew very well that even her parents were not comfortable realising that she had debased herself to the extent of camouflaging as a harlot and that she had the nerve to sleep with her father-in-law. She shook her head as if to clear it of her thoughts.

Looking back, it seemed she was another person, different from the one who had been so consumed with hate and spite for her father-in-law and yet driven by the will to receive a child from God at any cost. Was it the desperation for a child or the stigma of barrenness which she was anxious to strip off her name that drove her? She could not place it, yet she knew that the worst kind of despair in life was to be childless. As she strolled in the garden, she remembered the lonely nights she had spent in her mother's tent, nights when her mother would stealthily leave for her father's room, leaving her alone. She would act as if she were deeply asleep, yet with a knowing sting of jealousy, she imagined them coupling as lovers. How lonely and left out she used to feel. She missed her first husband, Er, and surprisingly, even the queer Onan would have been preferred than the lonely, helpless state she found herself in.

Chapter Twelve

THE TOWER OF EDAR

Judah saddled his donkey and rode towards his father's tent in Edar. He anticipated his father's surprise at their prospective meeting. After so many years! What would Jacob think? Would he welcome him? And what would he say to him when he heard his tales of woe, especially the tragedy with Tamar?

As he thought, he realised that he was just punishing himself with his mind-boggling thoughts when he was already on the way to meet his father and face whatever his fate would be.

He kicked the donkey to move faster as if he had made up his mind to face Jacob and get his predicament over and done with. He rode through the northern part of Canaan. The journey to Edar was a long one, it was about five days. His thoughts roved from his father to his brothers. They had all blamed him for the loss of Joseph and had excommunicated him from the family. Matters were made worse since he was the one in possession of the coat of many colours their father had made for Joseph. When Jacob saw Judah with the coat, he assumed that Judah had killed his little brother, Joseph, in the field.

This was because Jacob knew of Judah's personal endowment of strength. Judah had the strength that could crumble a rough piece of rock into dust, and it was a task to try to convince their father that a beast had killed Joseph. As he remembered the incident, Judah could not help but laugh at his foolish loyalty to his brethren by refusing to tell on them that he had to convince them to sell Joseph instead of letting them carry out their evil intention. He also realised that his years of separation from them had made him miss and yearn for their company despite their crookedness. Thankfully, his situation would make him pitiable, and they would attribute his suffering to divine retribution, justifying their false accusation.

He guided the donkey slowly down the slope of Edar to his father's tent. At first, nobody seemed to notice him, but his son Shelah recognised him at once from his gait and the familiar saddle on the donkey. Shelah had decided, on leaving his father in Chezib, to go to his grandfather, Israel. Although he had not known Israel, it was not difficult for Shelah to trace his abode in Edar by enquiring from the shepherds. So he had gone to Israel's tent on that fateful day when he decided to hide his anguish from his father. Israel had welcomed his grandson with open arms, although he could not help weeping over him with tears of joy that he could behold the son of Judah. Even though Shelah's reason for visiting his grandfather was vague, still Israel had given him lodging, trying as much as he could not to show his unease about the lad's flimsy excuse for coming without Judah.

Shelah felt completely at home in Edar with his cousins, and soon, he had completely forgotten his pains in Chezib. Now, seeing his father, he ran out of the tent to help Judah alight from the donkey to his father's chagrin. He took the donkey from him to the tethering shed, having greeted him and making an enquiry about everyone at home without an iota of resentment or sarcasm.

Judah could not help being surprised at the ease with which his son was concealing his earlier disgust at him. He found it odd that Shelah had left his maternal uncles in Chezib to pitch his tent with his grandfather Israel. From Shelah's attitude, it was clear to him that it would be out of place for him to conceal any of the happenings in his house because his son must have told Israel everything that had happened, which had culminated in his self-exile from home.

"Where is your grandfather?" Judah asked Shelah for want of freedom from his myriad of thoughts. Shelah pointed to Israel's tent, and Judah moved towards his father's abode. Israel gazed upwards at his son and could not believe his eyes as recognition hit him. He rushed out of his tent to greet him. He was glad, and his joy was boundless. As Judah stood before him, he embraced him and called out his name in the Hebrew tongue.

"Yehuda? Are these your eyes, my son?" Judah hugged his father's lean frame and held him to himself. He could not help the tears that flowed from his eyes as he held on closely to Israel as if his sanctification depended on it. After enquiring about Judah's family, Israel beckoned Judah to a seat and called for his wives to come and greet Judah.

Judah's mother, Leah, could not hide her joy at the sight of her son. This was her special son, the pillar and strength of his brethren. She knew him well; her praises of her God had endowed Judah with extraordinary grace and wisdom. When he left the family, there was an empty vacuum that no one could fill. His brethren were confused, having lost the true leadership of this rare species of a brother. The mothers missed his good and witty counsel. Leah ran towards her son and threw herself at him without caution. At the sight of his mother, Judah stood up with outstretched arms to wrap around her, minding her tender and frail body. She hugged and kissed him, rubbing his back and muttering her praises to Yahweh, who had preserved his token of praise.

"Yehuda!" she called aloud, "I never thought I would see you again, my son. When Shelah came to us and said he was your son, I found it difficult to believe. But for the striking semblance, I would have thought that a stranger was trying to defraud us.

Yehuda, Yahweh has kept His words to me by bringing you back to us alive. Let me go in to prepare your favourite meal before you tell the tales of your sojourn, my son."

Chapter Thirteen

THE CONFIDANT

Israel did not wait for Judah to eat before calling him into his tent to make his inquisitions.

"Is it well with you, my son? How are your family and the work of your hands? Shelah told me your wife died; what happened?"

Judah was only too glad to have an opportunity to vent his burdened soul. From his father's queries and earnestness, he realised that Shelah had not told on him. Except for the death of his wife, he had not divulged any of his family secrets to Israel. It was not as though he planned to keep the true situation from his father, but it gave him a good feeling to tell his father these things himself and witness his reactions firsthand.

Judah started by telling his father that he was sorry about coming short of his expectations. He told his father that before his visit to Edar, he had done a soul search of himself and realised that he had misjudged a lot of things in the past, relegating his responsibilities and making hasty and wrong decisions that had brought about life-threatening consequences. Judah decided to tell his father his own conclusion for his misfortune.

"Father, I should have stuck with you. I know that with all the accusations and pains for the death of Joseph, I am to blame. Still, I could have stood by you in your pain, but I allowed my brothers' threats to drive me out of the safety of my mother's guidance.

Instead, I found comfort in the hands of the Canaanites. I became estranged from you and your wise counsel. Here I am today, a widower with two sons of mine dead. Er, my first son, died after being married to his wife for just a few months. I gave the wife to my second son, Onan, to raise seed for Er, but Onan also died.

When I realised that the woman could have been responsible for the deaths of my sons, I quickly sent her back to her folk. This was the worst twist of my fate. The young woman expected me also to give her to Shelah, my youngest son. But I could not. So when my wife died from grieving for her sons, and I decided to go for my sheep shearing in Timnath, Tamar, my son's wife, tricked me. She dressed up as a temple prostitute, and I fell for her. Father, as I speak, Tamar is with child for me. She could not conceive for my two sons, but when I touched her just once, she became pregnant!"

Israel gasped in response to his son's sordid tale. He rubbed his hands on his face by reflex and held his son as if placating him would erase the enormity of his offence.

"Father, I have so messed up my life," Judah continued, "If Tamar was not a brave woman who was wise enough to take a pledge from me: my staff, signet and ring, which she showed as evidence, I could have caused the men of the land to burn her at the stake, and that would have further aggravated the matter. I cannot face my daughter-in-law anymore. My son, Shelah, is also angry at me, and he ran down here because of this. He did not even say a word when he left. He had grown and come of age and demanded for his bride, Tamar, which I denied him, thinking that it was for his good in order to spare his life. I wish I had explained things clearly to my only surviving son."

Israel coughed and cleared his throat before addressing his son. "Yehuda, I have listened to you carefully, and I know what you may be feeling; self-loathe, disgust and shame, but I am impressed with your evaluation of your misdeeds. You are not blaming anyone but yourself. You are also remorseful; I am surprised that you could show such bravery and courage to accept the blame over Tamar and also take her in to nurse her pregnancy. Not many young men of your stature would admit and account for such a cause. I am proud of you. Yahweh shall stand by you and keep your seed alive in Tamar to replenish you the loss of your two sons.

As for the death of your wife, I am sure the grief and shock of her sons' death had been unbearable for her. Take it as a man, for life is full of pains and shamefulness. We cannot explain or give reasons for things that we encounter. When I saw Shelah, I was astonished and deep in thought about his sudden arrival in my field. Still, the striking semblance to you and my longing for you did not allow me to probe about his actual situation and the reason why he came here without his parents. All the same, my son, take this as the challenge of life and just as you have searched your heart to find the reasons for your mishaps, try and make a decision on the best way to avoid a repeat of such complications in your life."

Israel spent a good time addressing his son that day, and he did not hesitate to repeat the story of his life; how he had deceived Esau to receive his blessing. Although Judah had heard this story before, it seemed to hold a special insight and interest to him this time as he could relate with the unease his father had felt when things started to get complicated for him in Paddan-aram with his grandfather, Laban. Israel also related the deaths of Deborah and Rachel, his beloved wife, and the pain of losing Joseph as great wounds to his soul which had permanently given him a peculiar stance on the affairs of life. He attributed his strength and forbearance to the love of Yahweh, who had been his stay. Israel told his son in clear terms that he was experiencing a new life as well as a new name, having had an encounter with the angel of Yahweh, who changed his name from 'an usurper' (Jacob) to 'Israel'. He also told Judah that for his humility and cool-headedness, which he had exhibited in handling his household affairs, he was on the right path to Yahweh taking over his life challenges and guiding him in his dealings in life.

Judah told his father that he had lost the desire to continue staying in Chezib and would love to pitch his tent with the rest of the family back in Edar. Israel gladly gave him his consent and blessings. Having unburdened himself to his father, Judah felt confident and sure-footed enough to visit his brothers in their private tents. Although he had mixed feelings on how they would receive him after these many years, yet his longing for them propelled him to go to his mother to seek counsel on how best he should go about it.

When he entered his mother's tent, he was greeted with the sweet aroma of his special meal. His mother was busy trying out several delicacies and snacks like dried dates, olives, *challa* and roasted lamb. Zilpah, his mother's maid, came to his mother's tent to greet him and to help her. Judah felt the warmth of his home once more as he ate and tasted all the meals placed before him.

After eating, he asked after his mother's sons – Reuben, Simeon, and Levi, his elder brothers, then Issachar and Zebulun and their only sister Dinah. He also enquired about the younger brothers Gad and Asher, which Zilpah had birthed for his father. Leah informed him that Reuben was a bit estranged as he had taken his father's wife, Bilhah, to bed, and to make matters worse, Israel had heard about it but had not said a word to Reuben.

Judah was dumbfounded; he could not utter a word. He knew that if he had not committed the same incestuous mess with Tamar, his reaction would have been quite different. He felt as though his wings were clipped to check his hasty judgment of others. This was really becoming a lifestyle now for him. First, he could not even blame his son Shelah for walking out on him and even when they had met briefly on his arrival in Edar; he was tongue-tied and unable to vent his anger or assumptions that his son must have gone ahead to expose his misdeeds.

Judah was becoming another man, slowly, gradually, but steadily. With the information about Reuben, Judah became conflicted on how to recount his own affairs with Tamar, how to inform his mother, at least for the mere reason that Tamar was expecting his child and would have to be admitted into the family in the long run when she put to bed. Judah swallowed hard and began his tale. Leah listened to her son and was at a loss for words at what she was hearing.

When Judah finished recounting his plight, Leah merely shook her head instead of talking. When she spoke, she asked Judah to bring Tamar to her tent to deliver her baby and insisted that Judah swear an oath to keep his words. Judah had no choice but to give in to ease the sour mood of his mother.

Chapter Fourteen

THE PRIDE OF A FATHER

As soon as Judah walked out of his father's tent to explore the other tents, Israel heaved a sigh of relief. It was as though he was dreaming. As he remembered his discussion with his son Judah, Israel recalled his own travail of soul on the night before he met Esau. Israel was familiar with the scourge of the Spirit and could feel within him that the hand of Yahweh was on Judah to prune and purge him for good. As a father, he had beheld his fourth son's rare ability to direct his brothers' affairs, although he was not the firstborn.

Judah had been wise and tactful, seasoning his words with salt before making any utterance. His counsel had always been pragmatic and realistic so that his brothers valued and held him in high esteem. Israel could not help but bow in thanksgiving to his God for ordering the steps of Judah back home. Instead of becoming bitter and self-justifying, he had become broken in spirit and willing to admit his faults. This, Israel decided, was more than a step in the right direction but rather an indication and a sign of his instinctive craving to set him as the pillar of his household.

His three eldest sons had failed him terribly. Simeon and Levi were wild and violent, lacking restraints, reason, and depth with their radicalism. He was not going to forget his grief in Shechem in a hurry, when those two caused his vulnerability and that of his wives and tender children. As if that was not enough, not even one of his sons could convince him about the whereabouts of Joseph, his favourite son.

The sound-minded Judah was not exempted in this, as he was very uncanny when Israel probed him about what had really happened to Joseph. He was certain that his son's disappearance was shrouded in a mystery that only Yahweh could reveal to him in His own time.

The more Israel appraised his sons one by one, the more pain he experienced as the act of Reuben and his young wife, Bilhah, stared him in the face. His first son had hurt him beyond the fabrics of his very being. How could Reuben have dared to touch his father's wife? It was an abomination, and Israel, at the time, had refused to say a word. Reuben had become dead to him. Israel had taken his firstborn out of all his business dealings from that time till the present. His lips had not uttered the name, 'Reuben'.

By his action, the young man had rendered Israel spineless and a joker, as the law of God would not let him strive with or kill any man. Now, with the glaring sanctity of Judah, Israel had hope that at least he had a coolheaded son who was capable of weighing his actions and admitting to his strengths and weaknesses. He could exhale at last that the promises that Yahweh made to him in Bethel saying, "I am God Almighty, be fruitful and multiply, as a nation and a company of nations shall be of thee and kings shall come out of thy loins," would be fulfilled. Judah was the manifestation of the promise; there was hope in Israel that one of his sons would be great yet. As Israel pondered upon God's promises, he could not help reminiscing on that last encounter he'd had with God.

He remembered Gods preservation of him and his children so that none of the Canaanites rose to attack him, his wives, flocks and children, even in the face of death and grief, was a sure sign of His faithfulness. Israel was unwavering in his faith in God, believing that whatever Yahweh promised, He would do for him. That deep trust and conviction kept him throughout his mourning for Rachel and helped him raise the baby, Benjamin, and his brother, Joseph. He could not also forget the resourcefulness of Leah, who cuddled the tender child and nursed him until he was weaned.

Israel was thankful for the outlets of mercy that God gave him as he coped in the plethora of grief that befell him. Looking back now as if it were yesterday, he realised that he had survived his trials for about twenty-two good years. This was a remarkable feat as he had never thought he would be able to adjust, especially when Reuben deprived him of his last hope of intimacy with Rachel's maid, Bilhah. He had to chew the bitter cud of accepting Leah as his rightful wife and giving her a place in his heart. It was as though that was what Yahweh required of him; to love his first wife and the mother of his oldest children.

As it were, he was left with no choice and was not ready to take another wife. Neither was he ready to start showing a preference for Leah's maid, Zilpah, over Leah. When this realisation occurred to Iarael, he had begun to adjust and treat Leah with respect and candour. Moreover, the peaceful atmosphere in the home had been a soothing balm to Dinah who was still hurting from the brutality of her brothers to the Prince of Shechem.

Although he could not love any woman like he loved Rachel, still, he was able to make Leah feel like a woman by comforting her, meeting her physical needs and parenting the tender sons of Rachel with him. He made up his mind to share his hopes on Judah as the heir apparent with Leah, and he knew that this would please her as she had also grieved openly for this 'special' son whom she had named her "Praises to Yahweh." Israel resolved that he would tell her in the night.

Chapter Fifteen

BROTHERS REUNION

When Judah finished his meal, he went looking for Reuben, his eldest brother, in his tent. Apparently, Reuben had heard of his coming into the camp from his nephews, who were Shelah's contemporaries, so he was not very surprised to see Judah walk into his tent. The two brothers embraced each other, forgetting the fray of their last meeting and the feud over their brother, Joseph. Reuben was a peace-loving man and temperate, and he was visibly happy to reunite with his mother's son.

"Yehuda, you have returned!" He cried out at the sight of Judah and held Judah to himself. After the greeting formalities, Judah sat down to talk with his brother. Judah realised that it was easier for him to face Reuben because of the issue with Bilhah, which had done a great deal to soothe his sense of worthlessness. He quickly told Reuben that he had come from very terrible and trying domestic problems at his home. He was deliberately laying bare his condition in order to help Reuben come out of his shell of self-condemnation.

As Reuben listened to the bit about his affair with the prostitute only to later discover it was Tamar, he could not help but laugh at Judah; jeering at him for not discovering the trap that Tamar had set for him. It was good to laugh again with his brother, Judah reasoned as he explained that he also had wronged Shelah who had been looking forward to marrying Tamar, which was why Shelah had left home in Chezib to come and pitch his tent with his grandfather. Reuben nodded and could only gaze at Judah calmly as Judah finished narrating his tales of woe.

He stared at Judah for a long time as if to assess his level of trust for the latter, and then he began, "I have not been so good myself, Judah. I fell for Bilhah and laid with her; she was always so kind to me. I did not know what came over me, and we were caught. Father has refused to say even a word to me."

For the first time since the incident occurred twenty years before, Reuben wept. Judah allowed him to cry out his pains. When he was done, Judah patted his back and assured him that he would talk to their father. Judah enquired about his other brothers from Reuben and asked after Dinah, their sister. Reuben told him that Dinah was still in Shechem and had left Edar for good, having been found with child from the Prince of Shechem. This piece of news cut through Judah like a sharp knife. He was distraught to hear the agony and reproach that his sister had to go through because of their earlier recklessness and inconsideration. Judah wished he could turn back the hands of the clock to reverse what they had done in Shechem. Distorted fragments of what had happened in Shechem flashed through his mind. Judah could have lost his life because of the war. He recalled the seven men who fought only him because they knew of his secret strength and had heard of how uncommon strength came upon him, and he smote forty-four men at once. He was still amazed at the incident even though it had happened more than two decades ago. He took time out to visit his brothers individually. As he toured and interacted with them, the nostalgia of returning to Edar overcame him, and he made up his mind to tell Israel of his feelings.

On returning to Israel's tent, Judah discussed his plan to return to Edar to his family. This was a welcome development, and Israel assured his son that there was room enough for him and his household. Israel also advised him to bring Tamar down to Edar to deliver her baby. Judah seized the receptive atmosphere to spend time with his father, asking probing questions about Yahweh. He had come to Edar for answers and so after the bubbling excitement of reuniting with his family, he made up his mind to choose a time to have a heart to heart talk with his father. Such an opportunity came on the second day of his visit to Edar when Israel asked him to go with him to his sheepcote in Mamre.

Judah dressed quickly and went with his father. He was astounded at the large flock his father owned. Israel was indeed very blessed of Yahweh. He was rich in cattle, sheep, camel and even goats. Judah observed that the settlement of his father's habitation had expanded from the Tower of Edar and beyond, even to Mamre. Although it was a desert land, the field was rich with pasture for the flock, and the land flourished with crops for food.

"Father, you are still very strong despite your limp. Tell me about your encounter with Yahweh again," Judah asked of Israel.

"As a young boy," Israel began, "my mother told me wonderful stories about Yahweh; His friendship with your great-grandfather, Abraham, and your grandfather, Isaac, being a child of promise. My mother, your grandmother, told me that my grandmother Sarah was a barren woman and married her husband for many years without a child. But Yahweh promised them that He would bless them with a special child through whom all nations of the earth would be blessed. Although the patriarch walked before God uprightly, the promise took a long time before it came to pass.

"One day, Abraham and his wife were in Mamre, and three men were passing by. Being a kind-hearted man, Abraham asked them to stop by for refreshments at his tent. The men came into his tent, and he asked his servants to prepare a sumptuous meal for the men. After the men had eaten, they called for Sarah, your great-grandmother and informed Abraham that the long-awaited child would be born the following year. This made them both laugh because Abraham was already a hundred years old, and Sarah was ninety.

"Despite their laughter, the three men told them that the said child would be born, and this child was my father Isaac, who you know. My father grew up as a precious child, loved and treasured by his parents, who kept building altars unto Yahweh wherever they went. It was one of those altars that answered me in my time of distress. I had run away from home when I offended my brother, Esau. My mother had misled me to wear Esau's cloak and cover my forearms with sheepskin to deceive my father, Isaac, that I was my brother, Esau. I succeeded in deceiving my father, and he blessed me with the portion of blessing he had reserved for Esau, his firstborn. When my brother later returned to my father with the savoury meal he had prepared for him as he demanded, and asked that he pour his blessings on him as promised. My father, shocked and confused, asked him who he was, querying him and insisting that he had already blessed him, not knowing that it was I who had usurped Esau's rightful blessing. My brother was wroth and threatened to take my life, but my mother heard his boast and told it to my father, who granted me his consent to go to your grandfather Laban in Paddan-aram because he was my mother's brother.

"This is how I met and encountered Yahweh: wearied and tired from my sudden flight from home, I slept, and suddenly I saw a vision of a ladder to heaven from the place where I laid my head. I heard a voice saying, 'I am the Lord God of Abraham thy father and the God of Isaac; the land whereon thou liest, to thee will I give it and to thy seed.' Yahweh promised to multiply my seed in the North, South, East and West. He promised to be with me and to fulfil all these promises. These words gave me great peace and assurance on my journey thenceforth. I was no longer afraid that my brother would catch up with me, neither was I afraid of wild beasts feasting on me on the way. I also pledged to him that if He took me to my destination and favoured me, I would serve Him all my life and give Him one-tenth of my income. I sealed this promise by raising an altar to Him at Bethel; that is why Bethel is a special and sacred place to me because it was the place of my first encounter with Yahweh.

From then on, my life has been guided and sustained by

Yahweh. When my uncle dealt treacherously with me by not paying me fair wages, my God prospered me. My parents experienced delay in childbearing for twenty years before my brother, and I were born. When I married your mother, she gave me sons in quick succession. Even though Rachel delayed in childbearing, she still gave me two strong sons, although Joseph is not alive Yahweh blessed me with a great flock of cattle, sheep and goats. I have camels and donkeys with faithful servants and maids. When your grandfather Laban became envious of my blessing, Yahweh instructed me in a vision to return to my father's house. I was afraid, but Yahweh promised that He would keep all my family and me.

My brother Esau was a wild man, a hunter given to great strength like you, Judah. I was afraid of him. I knew what he could do. Here I was, no longer alone, but with wives and young children, and I saw how vulnerable and susceptible to his vengeance I was. If he could not hurt me, what about my wives and children? He could also plunder the flock and take my servants to be his slaves.

"Despite my fears, Yahweh went ahead of me. He sent His Angel to bless me. He searched my heart and caused me to see my fault and who I truly was. I was a cheat, an usurper, and so rightly named. I knew what my mother did to my brother, yet I consented to deceive my father. When this reality hit me, I cried and wrestled with my old nature. I only prevailed by the Righteousness of God, and that morning, Yahweh changed my name to 'Israel'. He said He would take my physical confidence, for by strength shall no man prevail. I got this limp true to His words, and when I met my brother, Esau, he ran to me and embraced me instead of fighting with me.

My son, Yahweh, has been my comfort, strength, and guide; without His guidance, I would not be alive to see you now after all the terrible experiences I have had. When Rachel died, I thought I would die with her, but His hand sustained me. Even the death of Joseph has been bearable by His grace. When I am at my wits' end, He tells me, 'I am with you, and you shall prevail'. Yahweh is both shield and shade; He is enough, my son."

"Father, I am glad that you have painstakingly narrated this story of your life encounter again to me. But you know, this time, it is different and very important to me, as I can relate with you and understand why you always recount these experiences tirelessly. I have also experienced this inexplicable love of God. In fact, from the moment I admitted to my ill-treatment of Tamar, my life amazingly took a turn for the better. I no longer feel all the guilt and shame, but rather I am unburdened of even the grief that I wore like a cloak after the serial deaths in my house. Father, I have found comfort in Yahweh, and although He has not yet called my name or changed it, He has guided me in my dealings and organised my life to help me pick up the fragments of my being.

"When I asked Tamar to forgive me and to stay in my house, it was not by my ability. Ordinarily, I would have been defiant and unreasonable with her. Moreover, she would not have felt at home to stay with me, yet she surprisingly complied. I know that I have an uncommon will and physical strength, but this now seems useless to me as I have been weakened by too much grief and needed urgently to be strengthened in my soul. Ever since Tamar came into my home, an uncommon zeal and a sense of purpose have come upon me. It is as though I have become another man. I do not crave the friendship of the Canaanites anymore. I feel isolated even when I am with many of my friends. I seem to desire solitude with Yahweh more, I can sense His presence, but I long for Him to speak to me, and that is why I came. I need answers. I have so many questions. Who am I, father? Am I also a child of promise?" Jacob was stunned, though he smiled at Judah's exasperation. "Yes, you are, my son. As long as you are the offspring of Abraham, you are the child of promise in the flesh. You are right, Yahweh is with you. Although you have not heard Him speak, yet He speaks with you all the time, only you have been too busy to listen and talk with Him to discern His voice."

Chapter Sixteen

THE RETURN

The words of Israel were like drops of oil poured into Judah's chapped soul to soothe his aches; it was like clean water poured down the throat of a thirsty man. As he listened, he gulped the words like a healing balm to mollify himself. That night, when Judah got home from his father's sheepcote, he slept like a baby. There were no more troubling nightmares or nagging questions on his mind. One thing was dominant on his mind, though: to return to Chezib and bring Tamar to his father's settlement.

When he awoke the following morning, Judah quickly bathed, went to his mother's tent to greet her, and then greeted his father before saddling his horse to get back to Chezib. As he saddled his horse, he remembered that he had been too preoccupied with his quest for God even to have time for his son, Shelah. He realised that he would have to sit his young son down on his return to explain himself and apologise properly for his misdeeds. Having made up his mind thus, he made a fast dash to Chezib.

Machir was taken unawares by his master's sudden return,

although Judah had no clue about when he would come home. In his usual manner, he welcomed him with excitement even though he was a man of a few words and only spoke with his eyes. He quickly gazed at Judah's pursed lips but did not miss the radiance of his countenance; his master looked very healthy and relaxed. Machir wondered what could have happened to bring such a change of mood to his grieved master. He could not say anything to Judah except he was asked questions or given direct instructions, so he just collected the donkey, took it to its shed, and followed Judah into the villa.

"Is all well, Machir?" Judah inquired excitedly like a young lad. "How is everyone? Is the young woman well?" He threw the questions sporadically at his manservant. Judah was not a man to mince words, and so having enquired to know that everything was fine at the villa, he quickly told Machir of his plan to leave Chezib for good and with as many of his servants that would be willing to go with him. Judah stated clearly that he would not compel any of his servants to go with him. He also told Machir to call Tamar and her maid Anna to meet him for instructions.

Machir quickly called Tamar, who was so glad to hear that Judah had returned alive.

After the incident, the old man had acted so weirdly that his sudden disappearance had given her cause for grave concerns though she could not voice her fears to anyone. With news of his return, she found herself unnecessarily excited that he was alive and safe at least, if not for her, but for her unborn child. Although her pregnancy had advanced, she found herself moving with ease to meet Judah.

"Welcome home, father," Tamar called in greeting; Judah was glad to see her move with the agility of youth in her pregnancy. From her gait, he observed that her health was in an optimal state, and this made him glad. He asked her to sit and used the opportunity to thank Anna for faithfully carrying out the good job of looking after her. Judah cleared his throat and then told Tamar about his plan.

"I have decided to move back to Edar to live with my father and brethren in the family settlement. I have informed my father and mother of your condition, and they want you to have the best care and attention when it is time for your delivery. I have also seen the need to be with my family as my son, Shelah, is also with my father. I hope that this will not upset you or isolate you from your family, but I think in your best interest."

Although Judah knew that it would not be easy for Tamar to accept his decision, to his amazement, Tamar was elated. This she indicated by smiling broadly. It was such a welcome relief for her because she was almost bored to death in the old villa with no one but Anna to talk to, and so she quickly replied, "When, father?"

Her smile and question gave Judah joy. He had been full of trepidation at what her reaction to his decision would be since he was not ready to displease her in anyway, it gladdened his heart that she was inquisitive (and positively so), so he quickly answered, "As soon as you are ready to move," with a smile in his tone.

Machir and Anna just stood and watched the two of them in dismay. They both wore uneasy smiles because they were undecided about their fate. Moreover, they were still struggling to decide whether to move very far away from their native land with their kind master or stay jobless. Having settled with Tamar that he was on track, Judah was pleased and content. He was confident that Yahweh was ordering his steps back to his people and land. With Tamar's consent and lack of resistance, he was confident in doing whatever he needed to put in place to withdraw himself from the land of Chezib. When he finished talking to his servants and Tamar, he retired to his private chambers to execute the plans he had conceived in Edar. First, he would have to visit Timnath to assess the state of his flock there and to actualise the movement of the sheepfold down to Mamre. Also, at Timnath, he would have to inform Tamar's parents of his decision so that their daughter would arrange for proper farewell formalities with them. He had already decided to raise an altar to Yahweh in his villa. He was well aware that the land of Canaan would eventually be theirs as Yahweh had promised Abraham, so he decided to retain the house for future uses, just in case he had anything to do in Chezib.

Chapter Seventeen

FORGIVENESS

The prospect of seeing her parents brought a wave of uncertainty upon Tamar. She was not excited about the trip to Timnath yet she could not bring herself to confide in Judah, who was neither a husband nor a father, considering their awkward relationship. She also agreed with him on the need to let her parents know about her impending trip to Edar, where Jacob, Judah's father, lived, so there was no need for her to drag her feet or argue about it.

Moreover, she could not confide in Anna, her maid. As she made her way back to her quarters, she felt uneasy, as though someone was staring at her. She turned by reflex, only to see Machir hurrying after her. He had apparently been intending to catch up with her as a matter of urgency. Tamar stopped in her tracks and enquired, "What is the matter?'" Machir moved closer to her and said in a rehearsed tone, "You may not like me, I guess, but I want to tell you that you are a courageous woman, and I am so proud of you. If you ever need any help with moving to

Betshemesh, just be rest assured that I would be willing to help."

Tamar was taken aback by Machir's remark. She had not expected any form of personal or cordial comment from him. To her, it was alright for them to act as strangers because of her recent imbroglio. She had made her peace with his snobbish or mocking disposition. She could not help but smile to herself that Machir could extend an olive branch to her now that she was on the verge of leaving the villa. She was at a loss for words and merely nodded her consent.

She went to her room, and after resting her back on the armchair that Anna had provided for her, she decided to pack a few clothes into her overnight bag. She would have to spend just one or two nights with her parents since it was about three day's journey to her homeland. As she packed, she thought about Machir and his offer of help. It would not be bad to ride with him instead of going with Judah. The thought of going with Judah was very distasteful to her. Anna came into the room to help her pack, but Tamar thanked her, telling her that she had already packed a few clothes since she would only spend two days there. She also told Anna to prepare to go with her as she needed her company in case her health became challenging. Anna did not resist in any way and went quietly to get ready. Tamar went back to Judah to inform him about her desire to go to her parents' home with Machir.

Judah was busy sorting his plans for the sheepcotes. He would have to pay his workers reasonable wages, at least to last for a quarter, because he might not return for a long while. He would also need to take some cattle and start breeding in Edar. His head was filled with thoughts of the business of his flock that he did not hear Tamar come into his room until she called out in greeting. On hearing her, Judah turned and answered, asking her what had brought her back to him. Tamar did not hesitate to tell him that she would like to travel the next day and had prepared to go with her maid, Anna. He was glad that she was willing to work with him, although he was not even thinking about the time she was to move to her folks' place, so he asked rather casually, "What would you need for the trip?"

On that cue, Tamar blurted out at once, "Let Machir ride with us." Judah quickly responded, "By all means, he will, although it would have been more convenient for all of us to move at the same time, then we can drop you off at your parent's place on the way before I proceed to my sheepcotes. That way, we would save time and resources."

Tamar considered the options and nodded in agreement with him. Immediately she accepted his plans. Judah stood up to start packing his carryall bag. He said, "I will not delay our trip in any way. It would be better we all move tomorrow as you have decided. Do please call Machir for me on your way out." When Tamar went to Machir's tent, it was very strange for her to see the sudden change. It was the first time she was venturing into that wing of the villa. Before that time, she did not need to exchange pleasantries or even talk to anyone in Machir's household. So when Machir's wife saw her, she could not contain her curiosity; she had to look again to make sure the person who was walking towards her was Tamar.

"Is everything alright?" Rahab enquired. Tamar turned on the best of her charming smiles and said, "No, nothing is wrong.

Father wants Machir to come to him now. Could you get him to go immediately as it concerns matters of urgency, please?"

As Tamar talked, Rahab could not help but stare at her without listening to most of what she had to say. She did not know whether to stare at her or continue to talk to her. She could not take her eyes off the beautiful form before her, who was even lovelier with her full-blown pregnancy. Although Tamar knew about Rahab's eagerness to be friendly with her, she couldn't care less. She relayed her message and turned abruptly back to her room without a backward glance. She was not in the mood to make small talk with Machir's wife. As she walked towards her room, she wished they had known each other in better circumstances other than the present. She was also glad that she would not be travelling alone with Judah, especially on that particular route harbouring many bad memories for her.

Machir had heard the exchange between Rahab and Tamar, and as soon as Tamar left, he went quickly to Judah. He was sure that Judah was calling him in connection with the impending trip to Timnath. As he moved towards his master's tent, he thought about the Tamar he had known in the days of Er and Onan. At that time, Tamar was a very charming and gentle young woman, amiable and warm to everyone. He felt guilty for not being friendly and accommodating enough on her return to the villa. He reasoned that although she had descended low to trick his master into laying with her, she did not deserve to be scorned and mocked the way the servants in the villa did. He was relieved to have addressed her as he had earlier done, hoping that his confession would pave the way for better cordiality and possible friendship between her and his family in the future. He was thankful that his wife, Rahab, had not known Tamar when she married Er and later Onan, and so Tamar only had scores to settle with him and not with his wife.

As Machir neared Judah's room, he prayed that his master would discuss the trip since that would allow him to patch things up with Tamar. He rapped on Judah's door, and his master asked him in. Judah told him to make the donkey and the provender ready for they would be going to Timnath on the morrow and would need to take one more of his servants: Doeg, to saddle the women to Betshemesh, as Tamar would be visiting her parents. Machir pretended that the news of the trip was not pleasant to him, thereby concealing his anxiety and personal interest in the mission. Having succeeded in feigning his lack of interest, he casually asked Judah why he preferred Doeg to saddle the women instead of himself. To this, Judah simply waved his hand and said, "Whoever they prefer could go with them," as he was not ready to face Tamar's parents just yet.

Chapter Eighteen

SWEET HOME

Before they had parted ways at the bypass to Bethshemesh, Judah had asked his servants to stop with Tamar and her maid at a country Inn in Adullam for refreshment for the animals and themselves. As they dined, the servants left to feed the camels. Judah then told Tamar the reason he would not be going immediately with her to her parents. He assigned Machir to escort them and to leave the following morning to join them at Timnath. He told her that he would return in a few days to Betshemesh, with victuals that he would be able to gather in Timnath, where his sheepcotes were to make a ready present for her parents. Tamar was touched and very appreciative as she thanked him for always taking good care of her. They finished their patched cornmeal and then continued on their way.

Tamar's mother was busy drawing water from the well behind their tent when she heard the footfalls of camels coming very close to the tent. She dropped the bucket and peeked outside out of curiosity. She could not believe her eyes; Tamar was on one of the camels with another young woman and a man, whose dressing gave him away as a Canaanite. Dedan was overjoyed to see her daughter, whom she reluctantly left, at the urging of her husband, in Judah's house, not knowing what would become of her. So, Astarte had kept Tamar alive.

She exclaimed, "Tamar, are these your eyes that I am seeing my daughter? Have you come back to us at last?"

Tamar alighted from the camel and ran to embrace her mother. Anna came down and took their baggage off the camel. Tamar introduced Machir and Anna to her mother, telling Dedan, "They will be staying for a few days before Judah joins them back to Chezib."

Dedan took their stuff into the tent and called out for Reuel, Tamar's brother, who was working the land on the family field near their tent, to come home. Upon her enquiry, she found that Tamar's father had gone with his friend, Terah, to assist him in digging a new well. Reuel rushed back to meet Tamar and was very happy to see her after her embarrassing and hasty exit from home. Dedan handed Machir over to Reuel to take him to his tent where he would be comfortable in male company. Having done that, she quickly went to her kitchen to prepare a meal for her guests and to draw Tamar aside to get firsthand news of her affairs in Judah's house.

In the meantime, Tamar took Anna to a tent where she was to stay for the duration of the visit. Tamar told her to feel at home and change from her travel gear to a more comfortable dress. She showed her the stone-carved bathtub where she could have a bath and refresh. There was enough water in the reservoir at the washtub, so Anna would not need to go to the well outside to draw water for herself.

Having settled Anna, she went to her mother in the kitchen area of the tent. Her mother smiled at her warmly and said, "I cannot wait to ask you what life has been like with your selfish father-in-law. My dear, I hope you know and understand my restraint. I am sorry that I could not do much for you at the time, but I am glad that you can still find the courage to come to your home again."

Tamar smiled back as she gently sat on one of the kitchen stools, rubbing her protruding belly.

"Mother, I understand. Do not think I am ignorant of your and father's constraints towards me. I know how reproachful this whole incident was for you at the time. But mother, I really needed to have a child of my own to cuddle and to love. Judah was unfair to me when he refused to marry me to Shelah. I just hope you understand now that I can explain this to you," she said rhetorically, looking at nowhere in particular but gazing into space as she spoke.

Her mother listened attentively without interrupting her. When she was done, Dedan came to her and held her.

"My dear, I understand. I am not blaming you; neither is your father or your siblings. Shortly after you left, Erica heard the news and ran here to seek you out and take you to her place to stay with her, only to hear that Judah had admitted his fault and decided to take you in. In fact, we are fully behind you. I thank the gods that the pregnancy is progressing and you are well too. How is the Hebrew?"

Tamar sighed and looked down, hesitating before she could speak. Her mother urged her on, "Tell me. Is he too demanding?"

"No," Tamar shook her head, "On the contrary, mother, he cares for me and provides all the material comfort that I need. Even my travelling companion, as you can see, is to nurse and answer to me. He caters for needs, but he does not come to my tent. He does not come near me as a woman." At this point, she broke down and wept. She sobbed and racked her grieved soul for a long while. Dedan looked at her daughter and did not know what to say at the moment. She just allowed her to weep until she was done, then she cradled her face and used her veil to wipe her tears. Very quietly, she enquired about Shelah. This made Tamar resume her weeping. She answered in between sobs that Shelah left the house the next day after the incident because he was angry at his father. She told her mother of her ordeal; how in a tense and hostile environment with almost everyone hating her, the only friend she had who cared about her was Shelah. But then, he left because his heart was broken, and Judah had refused to take emotional responsibility towards her to comfort her and meet her intimate needs as a woman. As she emptied her soul before her mother, she felt relieved, especially after opening up to free herself from the pains she had harboured in her heart.

Dedan was worried that perhaps Tamar had left Judah's house to their home for good, so she asked, "So is this why you are back here?"

Tamar shook her head and blew her nose to clear her voice as she explained the reason for her visit to her mother. Dedan sat down to hear the explanation; that Judah was actually on a trip but had come to pass some time at Timnath, at his sheepcotes there, and would return to see her parents in a few days.

She told her about Judah's plan to take her to his parents in Edar for confinement. His parents had requested for her there so that they could take proper care of her. Dedan sighed in relief as she went to check the food that she had been cooking.

Then slowly and quietly, she began to tell her daughter what was on her mind. "Tamar, you were wrong in your choice of action. If you told me that Judah was passing this way or was coming to Timnath, your father and the elders would have intercepted him at the gate to inquire about the way forward concerning your marriage to Shelah. If he did not give them a favourable answer, then we would have known what to do to free you so that you can marry another man. You were too hasty, and you allowed bitterness to becloud your judgment. How could you sleep with your husband's father? What were you thinking? Now he is so ashamed of himself, and maybe their God will not permit him to take pleasure in you, and that is why he is being so generous, doing everything else to make it up to you. Please take him for what he can be for now and concentrate on your well being and that of the baby. After your child is born, I am sure; things will sort themselves out."

After this candid submission, Dedan quickly dished out a sumptuous meal of *shakshouka* and *ganoush* for them. Tamar had missed her mother's cooking. In Judah's house, she had no choice but to eat whatever was available. She called out for Anna as she put large portions of the *shakshouka* in a flat plate for herself.

As they ate, Machir and Reuel joined them. They talked about the weather, and the harvest, which was an improvement from the previous year. Reuel was a tiller of the soil, so he gave them firsthand information on crops like barley, maize, and sorghum. Tamar asked Reuel about Deliah; since she was too tired to go out to look for her as it was already sunset; she was surprised that Deliah was not curious in her usual easygoing nature to visit to know who the latest visitors were in their house. Reuel told her that Deliah left for Adullam as soon as Tamar left Betshemesh for Chezib. Tamar was so disappointed as she had so much to say to her since they had not met each other for a long time. She wished her situation were different so that she would have the liberty of going to look for her even in Adullam, but in this case, she was bound by Judah's instruction and the short time she had to stay with her parents. Machir munched away in silence, waiting for an opportunity to address Tamar after dinner. After dinner, he seized the opportunity by thanking Tamar's mother, saying that her daughter was also an excellent cook; he could remember the savoury meals that were credited to her in the villa.

At the unexpected compliment, Tamar smiled in surprise and a mixed feeling of pride and nostalgia for those days of her true worth and confidence, borne out of the love and acceptance of her first husband Er. As she turned to walk away, Machir moved up close and held her hand, telling her not to be in such a hurry to retire to her tent, but she could at least show them around their neighbourhood. Tamar shook her hand free from his grip and declined, giving the excuse that she needed rest due to her condition. However, she promised to avail herself when her father returned later in the evening.

Chapter Nineteen

A RENEWED MIND

It was a smooth ride from Ena'im Temple to Timnath, and although memories of his involvement with Tamar surfaced on his mind as he rode past, he felt no guilt since his conscience was clear now that he had confessed his sin. However, he could not shake off the curiosity from his mind; of why Tamar deceived him and how she could have known that he was coming that way. He wanted to know how she had planned to deceive him as she did. Ordinarily, these are issues that he could have extricated from her if they were contemporaries or if she was his wife and not his son's wife; but he could not. He just realised that the people around him and her people were watching him and reporting his every move.

This realisation came as a check to his life and dealings. All of a sudden, it became clear to him that Tamar's people were unhappy with him for not keeping his promise to marry Tamar to Shelah. He was thankful nonetheless that Tamar had been that brave and wise to take the pledge that had become a 'saving grace'.

Her death could have sparked a serious rift between him and her people. He was at peace that Tamar was content to remain in his house and now was probably at her parent's home, and things were gradually returning to normal again.

Although he would not be able to marry Tamar, it would not be out of place to still redeem his promise of giving her to Shelah so that she could raise an heir to Er, his late firstborn. That way, both Tamar and Shelah would be happy, and Judah could remarry in future.

Judah shook his head as if to clear it of his thoughts as he galloped towards Timnath. The sun was going down. He had already planned to spend the night on his threshing floor, where he had a lodge prepared and ready. This was where he usually spent his nights in the times past. He moved towards the lodge where he would rest for the night with his servants and then prepare to work on his farm.

Early the following morning, Judah rose to visit his manservant, Zechariah, who was the overseer of all Judah's businesses in Timnath. He had already sent words to him in the evening of his arrival to let him know that he was in town, so Zechariah was expecting him. In his usual manner, his wife, Ruth, and three daughters had prepared breakfast of fresh-baked bread and herbs sauce for Judah as he sat in front of his servant's tent.

He told Zechariah of his plans to extend the farm to Edar, where his father Jacob was staying as he ate. He did not want to tell him of his plan to leave Chezib ultimately, since his close relationship with Zechariah would demand that he state his reasons. Judah had about eighteen sheepcotes in Timnath. He had a cattle ranch, goats and lambs and a good collection of pigeons which fetched him good proceeds in the nearby market. He told Zechariah to send word to all the shepherds and shepherd boys not to take the sheep out until they had done stocktaking and headcounts of each sheep in the cotes. Records of sales from the previous sheep shearing exercise the last time Judah visited was to be brought to the table for reckoning. Zechariah did as he had instructed, and before Judah arrived at his tent that morning, the herdsmen were already waiting.

Machir sighted Judah and Doeg afar off as he rode towards them, although they could not see him since Timnath was a busy community where sheep business and other farming activities bubbled. With different people riding on donkeys, camels and asses, it was not easy to make out who was who, but knowing the location of the farm lodge, Machir could make out Judah and Doeg trying to mount the camel as they set out to the farm settlement. On his part, he had awoken quite early to thank Reuel for his warm company and to leave word for Tamar's mother and Tamar that he had left. As he rode, he reminisced on the conversation they'd had that night with Tamar's parents and brother. It was not a wonder that Tamar was such a goodly young woman; the apple, it is said, does not fall very far from the tree. Tamar's mother was a woman of high morals and virtue. They were Israelites, although they worshipped the Canaanite gods of wood and stone. They talked late into the night about his master's insensitivity and inconsideration towards Tamar and her parents. Machir tried to defend Judah, asserting that the poor man had been afraid for the life of his only surviving son, especially when his wife died also.

Shannon, Tamar's father, saw reason with Machir and reiterated that he had no hard feelings towards Judah, especially as he had agreed to own up to Tamar's 'senseless risk', as he called it. Machir seized the opportunity to ask Tamar to forgive Judah and himself. Tamar smiled at this and said she bore him no grudge. Having unburdened himself to the best of his ability before Tamar's family, Machir took his leave to retire, knowing he had a busy schedule the next day.

As he waddled through the sheep market towards Judah's farmland, the market's noise was deafening, and it made riding cumbersome, so he disembarked and strolled with the camel through the maze of buyers and sellers in the busy market. He could not resist the fresh fruits of the season; pomegranates, berries, olives and apples lit the vegetable stands. He stopped to buy some raisins for his wife, knowing that he might not come this way again because they would be returning in a group. Timnath was a rich agricultural settlement, so the fruits on display were cheaper than the ones sold in Chezib. He soon arrived on the farm and headed for Zechariah's tent.

Judah addressed them about the business of the day and assigned chores to them while he hastily helped himself to the delicious breakfast set before him. He was glad that Machir had arrived very early, so he assigned the eighteen sheepcotes between the three of them; six to Zechariah, six to Doeg and the last six to Machir. They were to give situation reports of animal population, mortality rates, animals due for shearing, and the feeble ones to be taken out. It was necessary to carry out this sorting early in the morning before the animals got hungry and thirsty for their daily pasture.

Having instructed his servants on the business of the day, Judah felt free and purposeful. He hadn't felt that fulfilled in a long while. He had renewed energy as he rode his favourite donkey, which was kept in the farmland for his tours of the fields. He was a free man again. He had forgotten the grief for his wife and the nagging shame of his affair with Tamar. His journey to Edar and his relief to know that Shelah was safe also took all the burdens and fear from him. He urged the donkey forward with the agility of youth, and the wind gushed through his thick hair. He looked forward to a very productive day with his herdsmen and flock. With such a gay spirit, Judah was able to take stock of the various activities. The reckoning of the multiple flocks was very encouraging, and the mortality rates were very low. He greeted his herdsmen with joy as they gave him the progress reports of their different divisions.

In each sheepcote, he had two attendants; one for the goats' pen, which was separated from the sheep pen. There were shepherds that Judah hired to manage different aspects of the animal affairs, from shearing to handling of the produce on the farmland gardens, where the women worked tirelessly to plant and tend the crops of the various seasons. Most of the workers had married in the course of working together, so it was a community of close ties working together towards the same goal. Judah sat on a makeshift chair from a trunk of an oak tree whilst sorting out the parent stock that Zechariah had carefully selected to be taken to Edar with his other servants. He was happy with the level of work that they had done on the farm.

They continued with the bookkeeping the next day. The sheep

shearers took out the ones that needed shearing, while Zechariah and Machir compiled the wages to be paid to the workforce for the next quarter as Judah had proposed. At the evening tide, they were treated to roasted lambs and goats' broth. Ruth roasted maize for them, and the young maidens danced in the firelight to entertain them while they ate. It was a very eventful and wonderful evening well spent in Timnath.

Chapter Twenty

SISTERS

Tamar's father, Shannon, slept contentedly for the first time in months. As a man, he had learnt to hide his tears and sorrows; he did not have much choice than to be quiet and wait for his daughter's fate. One thing made him hopeful; the fact that she was still alive and had been saved from the reproach of being burnt for her presumed adultery. To come home to see her hale and hearty was a greater relief to him. When Judah's servant begged Tamar for her forgiveness, that was the climax for Shannon, as he felt that it could only mean that perhaps, Machir believed that she would become the Lady of Judah's household.

With such thoughts and Judah's impending visit as Tamar had informed him, Shannon's age lines had disappeared, and as he woke up the following day, he found himself humming to an old fable song. He had to prepare for Judah's visit by setting apart some choice farm produce as gift tokens for him and choosing the best of his calf to be slaughtered for food for his visitors. He called his wife, Dedan, and gave instructions for the preparation, gave her money for supplies directed what drinks would be served to Judah and his company while he went to the field with Reuel to get the things from the farm. It was a good thing Judah was coming in two days, so he had ample time to put things in place.

Tamar had taken her mother's counsel in good faith, and her countenance was not sad anymore. She moved with ease and boldness once more in her house and the neighbourhood. She took Anna around their home gardens and took delight in picking the inviting vegetables from her mother's garden. Anna was good company and could not help but relax in Tamar's country home. They ate the apples, the pomegranates and pears that were so abundant. Tamar also stole the time to visit Erica and Joella.

Erica thought that her eyes were playing tricks on her when Tamar showed up at her doorstep. The absence had made Tamar's ties with her sister more tender. They hugged and kissed each other as they shed tears of joy. Erica exclaimed, "Oh, my sister, I never knew I would see you again. I couldn't come to Judah's house; Carmi would not have permitted it. I heard what happened, and by the time I got home, you had already gone."

Tamar tried to calm her down. Saying the worse was over and that she was looking forward to giving her either a niece or nephew. On that lighter note, Erica eased up on her emotion.

Joella raised her little hand to Tamar to carry her, and Tamar gladly bundled her and showered her with kisses. It was obvious that the girl had missed her *Aunty Yamar'* as she called her from her toddler chatter. It was a very heartwarming reunion for them.

She stayed in Erica's house for a greater part of the day, and when it was time for her to go, her sister showered her with gifts of clothes for her and the expected baby. She obviously wanted a niece, so she gave her most of Joella's outgrown babywear. She also gave ner new shawls and wraps with matching beads to adorn herself. Tamar was so happy, and it dawned on her that Erica loved her despite their sibling brawls and disagreements. Erica promised to come to their home on the day of her departure from Bethshemesh to bid her farewell.

As they bade each other goodbye, Joella stuck to Tamar and refused to let go, screaming, *"Aunty Yamar, Aunty Yamar!"*

This brought tears to Tamar's eyes as she held on to her and promised to get Erica to bring her when her baby or babies were born. Erica had to forcefully snatch her weeping daughter off Tamar so that they could leave. Anna, who was a quiet person, just tagged along without interfering in the two sisters' reunion. She reasoned that they needed the privacy so that they could bask in each other's company as the time was short.

It was already dusk when they arrived at Tamar's house, so the two joined Dedan in the kitchen to prepare the evening meal. Soon, they ate and retired to bed for the night.

EPILOGUE

Judah visited Bethshemesh and was warmly welcomed by Shannon and Dedan, Tamar's parents. He brought ten donkeys, ten calves, twenty goats, and twelve sheep carried by his servants from Timnath. He also came with baskets of apples, corn, wheat and barley. Shannon received them with gratitude from Judah and welcomed him to his home. He thanked Judah for his care for Tamar and his kindness in allowing her to visit them. He did not want to dwell on the fracas of the past and only mentioned that Judah was a man of integrity, truly an Israelite without guile, as he had demonstrated by owning up to his fault and saving his daughter's life.

In reality, Shannon posited that he was proud to be identified with Judah as a fellow Israelite. Judah listened with rapt attention as Shannon spoke before his wife and Tamar, who were the only ones to eat with him (the servants had been given a separate shed where they were served with delicacies). Erica kept to her words by coming with her daughter to help in the feast that Shannon prepared for his august visitors.

In response, Judah told Shannon that it was not his intention to have kept Tamar away from Shelah for that long, but his fear, stemming from the serial deaths in his family, had completely taken him out of his wits. Although his affair with Tamar was embarrassing to him, he would never have had any dealings with her if he had any clue to who she was. He also appealed to them to look at the blessing in disguise as God had kept her healthy and the pregnancy was progressing. He finally decided to let the cat out of the bag by informing them that his main reason for bringing Tamar to visit them was to let them know that his father, Jacob, and his mother, Leah, were now aware of the circumstances and they had advised him to bring Tamar down to Edar where she would be nursed properly during her confinement. He made them see reason with him as his wife, Sheena, had died and there was no elderly woman around to play the role of tending Tamar and the infant when she would put to bed.

Tamar's parents were relieved to know how meticulous and thoughtful Judah had been in handling the matter, and thanked him in earnest. They also expressed their desire to visit when Tamar's time was due. Having eaten and discussed all that was relevant to his visit, Judah rose and thanked Shannon and his wife for their generosity and hospitality. He asked Shannon to send word to his servants to make ready for their departure as he nodded to Tamar. Shannon also called his son and servants to make his gifts ready for Judah. He presented him with five fat calves, seven colts, five goats and baskets of raisin and dates.

Judah accepted these gifts with gratitude and called for some of his men who had to return to Timnath to begin to head out, while Machir and Doeg took the gifts and started on their way back to Chezib. In Chezib, they rested for two days from their long journey, then they packed up and made ready on the third day to return to Edar. So, Judah returned to Jacob, his father, and Yahweh, his God, from the company of the Canaanites and from Hirah the Adullamite.

The sceptre shall not depart from Judah, nor a lawgiver from between his feet, until Shiloh comes, and unto him shall the gathering of the people be...